NINE MAN'S MURDER

XXX
XXX
XXX

ERIC KEITH

Ridgewood, NJ

Publisher's Note: This is a work of fiction. Names, characters, places, and incidents either are the product of the author's imagination or are used fictionally, and any resemblance to actual persons, living or dead, events, or locales is entirely coincidental.

10 9 8 7 6 5 4 3 2 1

Book design: Emily Marlowe
Cover design: Pamela Gelbert

Ransom Note Press, LLC
P.O. Box 419
Ridgewood, NJ 07451

Library of Congress Cataloging-in-Publication Data

Keith, Eric, 1951-
Nine man's murder / by Eric Keith. — 1st U.S. ed.
p. cm.
ISBN 978-0-9773787-7-7 (pbk.)
1. Private investigators—Crimes against—Fiction 2. Vacation homes—Fiction.
I. Title. II. Title: 9 man's murder.
PS3611.E368N56 2011
813'.6—dc22
2010034858

I dedicate this book to my wife Marcia,
without whom I would not be possible.

THE PLAYERS

CARTER ANDERSON
Employee in his brother Damien's detective agency. Has lived his life in his brother's shadow. But he is about to step out.

REEVE ARGYLE
Son of poor Italian-American parents, he is a bodyguard hunted by a crime lord for a betrayal he did not commit. But is he the hunted or the hunter?

HATTER CATES
Best-selling author of violent supernatural thrillers and spokesman for the occult. Hatter believes the dead return to avenge their deaths. The question is: Do they have help?

JILL CONSTABLE
A home health-care nurse. Romantically involved with Bryan West fifteen years ago. The secret she shares with Amanda Farrell is one she is willing to die for. But is it one she is willing to kill for?

JONAS CRUZ
Formerly a business partner of Bryan West. Son of migrant farm workers. Has a secret to hide. To keep it buried, will others have to be buried with it?

AMANDA FARRELL
Prosecutor for the district attorney, building a case against the employer of her former lover, Reeve Argyle. To what lengths will she go to get a conviction? And to what lengths will she go to cover it up?

GIDEON LANE
A wheelchair-bound priest defrocked after a "misunderstanding," Gideon is searching for the culprit responsible for his condition. Do his religious beliefs include "an eye for an eye"?

BENNETT NASH
A freelance smuggler on the run from the law. How far will he go to stay one step ahead?

BRYAN WEST
Owner of a detective agency. Former business partner of Jonas Cruz. Romantically involved with Jill Constable fifteen years ago. On a crusade to avenge a family tragedy, and willing to bend the rules. But how far?

Moon's End

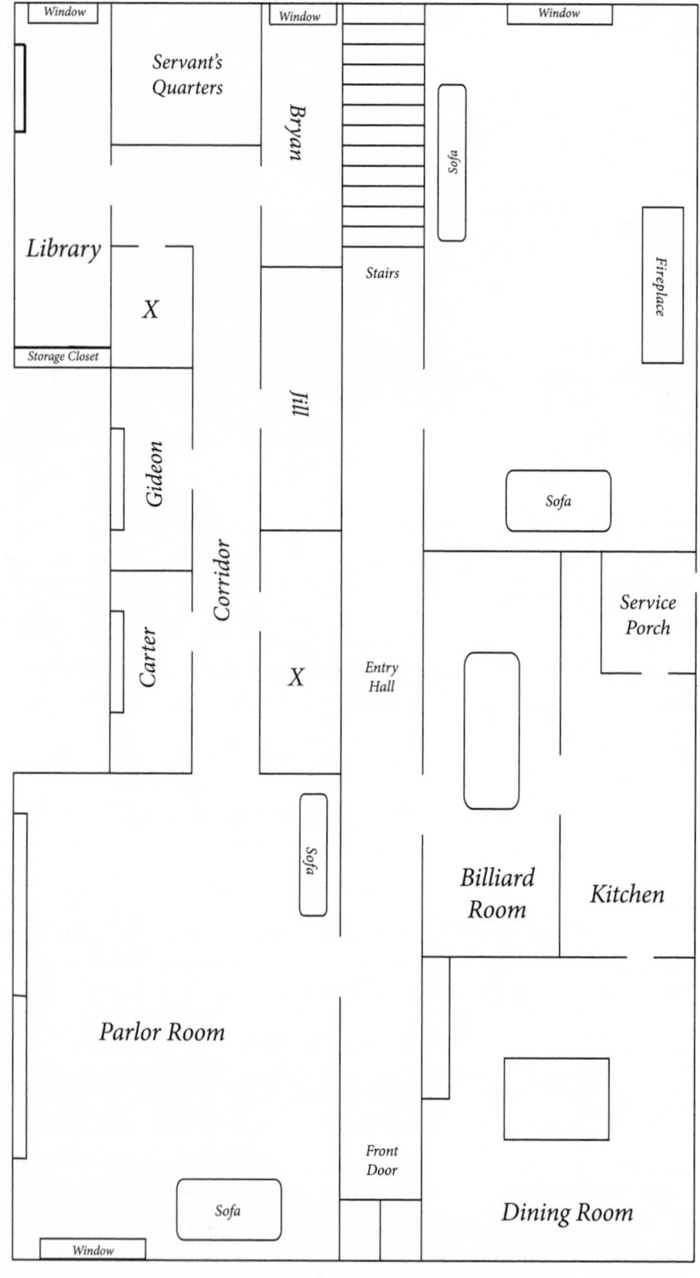
Window
Servant's Quarters
Window
Bryan
Window
Sofa
Library
X
Stairs
Fireplace
Storage Closet
Jill
Gideon
Sofa
Corridor
Service Porch
Carter
X
Entry Hall
Sofa
Billiard Room
Kitchen
Parlor Room
Front Door
Sofa
Dining Room
Window

Floor Plans

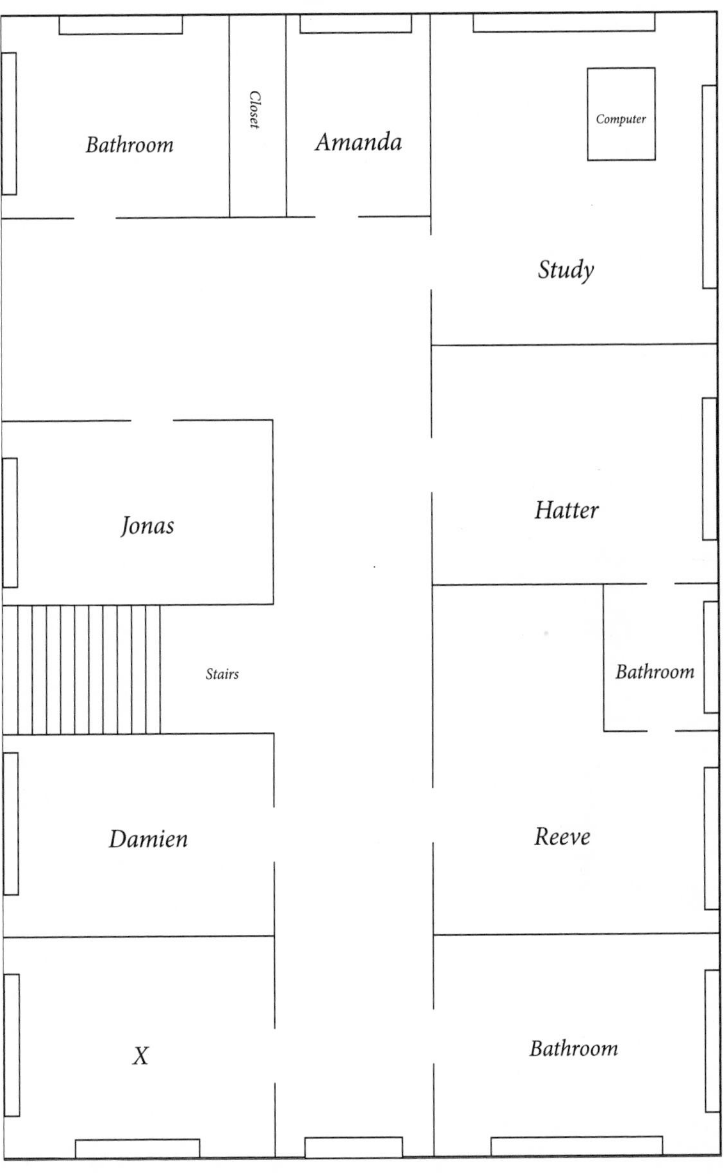

⇦ First Floor

⇧ Second Floor

X: Unoccupied

TWENTY-SIX YEARS AGO

Los Angeles Times

September 1

LOS ANGELES, CALIFORNIA—The four-year-old daughter of District Attorney Nathaniel West disappeared yesterday from her Santa Monica home. Police are treating the disappearance as a kidnapping, though as of this time no ransom demand has been received. West, a candidate in the upcoming mayoral election, has declined comment. A spokesman for Mr. West says that the district attorney will be suspending all campaign activities as the search for his daughter continues. There is yet no word as to whether Mr. West will drop out of the race.

Los Angeles Times

September 5

LOS ANGELES, CALIFORNIA—Four-year-old Priscilla West, daughter of District Attorney and mayoral candidate Nathaniel West, was found yesterday in an abandoned tobacco shop in the Crenshaw district. The girl was kidnapped from her Santa Monica home four days ago. Doctors have no comment concerning Priscilla's physical condition, citing the need for further examination. No arrests have been made. Police say they are continuing to investigate the kidnapping but will release no details, except to speculate that the kidnapping appears to have been a professional job.

Part One

xxxxxxxxxx

Invitation to the Game

THE PRESENT

December 12

THE RAILROAD STATION was deserted. Not a soul in sight. Bryan West had arrived before the others, it seemed.

What if no one else showed up? No, the invitation had been too intriguing to pass up. Still, it was over three hundred miles from Los Angeles. The sun had beckoned after him when Bryan had left the hub of southern California this morning; here glowering thunderheads were strung across the sky like No Trespassing signs. Best to wait inside.

It would be a well-earned vacation. Bryan had been working too hard, pushing himself to build an empire out of the bankrupt carcasses of his competitors. A ruthless game, but it had to be played.

Absently he fingered the knotted cord dangling from his neck, the necklace Prissy had made for him. If it were not something that could be damaged in the shower, it would never leave his body at all. Was it only yesterday he had last seen her? Thursday … yes. Twice a week he saw his sister, regular as clockwork.

We were all victims of the kidnapping, Bryan thought. *Mom. Dad. Priscilla. Me.*

Bryan glanced around the large, ghostly station. He was alone.

He slipped the note from his jacket pocket and read it once again with a frown. Typed. No clues as to the author. All his adult life he had been investigating threats like this to other people; but now that it was personal, he understood why his clients had always been so unnerved.

The unexpected sound left him little time to thrust the note back into his pocket. A creaking of metal and slow muffled footsteps echoed behind him.

"Move and you're dead." The footsteps drew nearer. "Now raise your hands and turn around. Slowly."

With arms raised, Bryan turned, green eyes faintly aglow, to confront the muzzle of a small silver handgun.

Bryan studied his assailant. Taller than Bryan, with a wiry frame. Sleek black hair swept carelessly across a tawny forehead, wrinkled with care and browned as much by the sun as by his Latin heritage. Cool brown eyes with a hunted look, like a man running from something.

"Well, if it isn't the late great Bryan West," said the newcomer.

Bryan glanced at his wristwatch.

"Actually, I'm a bit early."

"Still the same old wise guy. Just like when we were partners. Coolheaded, always one step ahead of your adversary. Fiercely competitive, to the point of stealing clients from rivals."

"Funny, you never complained when my tactics failed. Only when they worked." Bryan stared at the gun. "Do you really need to point that thing at me?"

"I do if I want to shoot you."

The explosion muffled Bryan's protest before he could utter it.

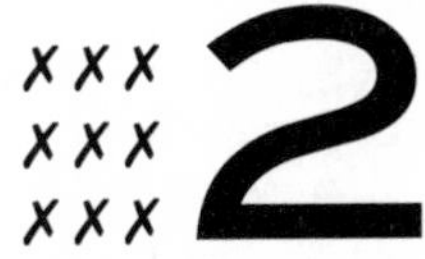

Bryan West's twisted form lay lifelessly on the railroad station floor. Beside him, a shadow shook its head.

"You're still an unconvincing actor."

Bryan lifted his head. "You're still a lousy shot, Jonas."

Jonas Cruz emptied the cartridge from his weapon.

"Oh, I didn't miss." He held the bullets in his outstretched hand. "Blanks."

Bryan took them from Jonas, studying them briefly before depositing them absently in his jacket pocket.

"Remember the last time we used that trick?" Jonas asked. "It saved both our lives."

One of their many escapades during their partnership.

"So," Jonas continued, "is this reunion going to be business or pleasure?"

"Business?"

Jonas glanced around the empty station. "Carter and Damien will both be here." He waited in vain for a reaction. "Have you said anything yet? To either of them?"

"Not yet."

"Do you plan to … at the reunion?"

"I haven't decided."

"I see." Jonas lowered his voice instinctively. "Jill will be here, too, you know. I suppose you know about Lakeview."

"Yes, I know."

Bryan began pacing in front of the broad train station windows. "Do you think anyone else will show up?" he asked.

"If training counts for anything. The invitation *I* received was too enticing for any trained detective to pass up. What do *you* make of it?"

"Well, it wasn't so much the invitation that intrigued me, as the envelope. That L.A. postmark—"

Something outside the window stopped Bryan's tongue. "Well," he said, "I think we're about to get some answers."

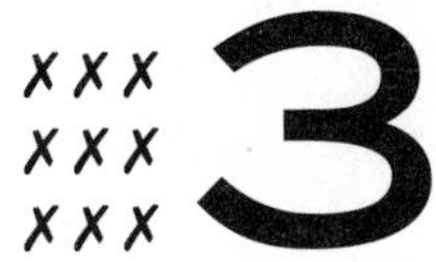

Carter Anderson watched the two men emerge from the train station.

"At last," Jonas said. "Someone who can tell us what this is all about."

Carter's frown formed before he could suppress it. "Sorry, but Damien never mentioned a word about this—to me, anyway. I'm as much in the dark as you."

"Isn't this rather unlike Damien?" Bryan asked. "He comes to Moon's End to be alone."

"Every year at this time, for two weeks," Carter confirmed. "That's why he bought Moon's End—to get away from everyone." Carter held up his invitation. "Which is what makes this invitation so odd. I've never known my brother to do anything like this."

"Damien *sent* you an invitation?" Jonas regarded Carter through narrowed eyes. "He didn't just tell you about the reunion?"

"Not even a hint. I got my invitation in the mail."

"You'd think he would have said something to you," Bryan said, as puzzled as Jonas. "You work with him every day."

But it wasn't just the idea of Damien sending Carter an invitation that was odd. It was the invitation's tone, as well. It didn't sound like Damien. It was too … theatrical? Melodramatic? Formal?

"I tried calling Damien at Moon's End," Bryan said, "but all I got was static."

"Probably a downed phone line. Must have taken out the Internet, as well. I tried sending him an email, but it didn't go through. If the phone is out, the Internet won't work, either." Carter shook his head. "Not that Damien would have bothered to turn on his computer."

But Carter and Bryan had not been the only ones trying to reach Damien. Someone had called for him at the office three days ago. Anna had taken the call. Didn't leave his name, Anna had told Carter. Asking when Damien had left on his vacation.

And that wasn't the only strange call the Anderson Detective Agency had received recently. Two months ago someone had called, asking Anna questions about Damien's graduates fifteen years ago. Carter's graduating class.

Why would anyone want to know about them?

4

She was not the first to arrive. Three others were already there, loitering outside. The tall, gaunt one with the careworn face and short, conservatively cut hair, starting to thin: That had to be Carter. With him were Jonas and Bryan. It was not as if she hadn't known this was going to happen.

"Jill," Jonas called out. "It's good to see you."

He took her hand in both of his. Quickly she withdrew it and stepped backward.

"Jill Constable?" Carter said. "Wow, Jill, you look great."

Jill risked a sidelong glance at Bryan. He stood staring at the ground. The silence was painfully awkward.

Did Bryan know about Lakeview? Bryan seemed to know everything. Well, why should she care? After what he had done, why did it matter what he thought?

Nonetheless, she would stay away from him. And Jonas. She would stay away from both of them.

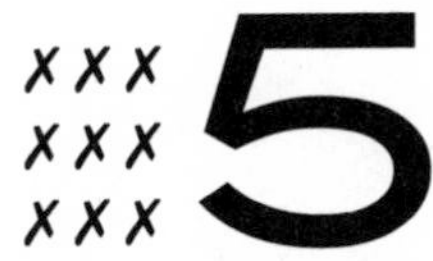

5

Office of the Los Angeles District Attorney
Update
November 25

Re: Evidence recovered from Cahuenga warehouse fire

Yesterday a fire burned to the ground a suspected counterfeiting base of operations for reputed crime lord Antonio Capaldi. Capaldi is the subject of an eight-year investigation by Deputy District Attorney Amanda Farrell. Ms. Farrell has been accumulating evidence of illegal activities by the Capaldi ring: in particular, a counterfeiting operation.

The current theory is that Capaldi got wind of rumors that investigators were closing in on his operation and torched his own warehouse in order to destroy any incriminating evidence. Fortunately, a close examination of the site uncovered a silver key. The key's unique design made it possible, through painstaking canvassing of locksmiths in the Los Angeles area, to identify the manufacturer. The key proved to be custom made for a special lock—on a drawer in Antonio Capaldi's office.

A warrant to search the office gave investigators the opportunity to unlock that drawer, in which they found a ledger filled with coded entries. It is hoped that when cryptographers have succeeded in deciphering the entries, the ledger will provide evidence of Capaldi's counterfeiting activities, and possibly other crimes as well.

The ledger is currently being held in the evidence locker of the downtown headquarters of the Los Angeles Police Department.

☙☙☙

Excerpt from Preliminary LAPD Report
November 28
Re: Attempted theft from evidence locker

Yesterday, a coded ledger possibly linking crime lord Antonio Capaldi to dozens of crimes, including the arson at his suspected counterfeiting lab that resulted in one known death, was the object of an attempted theft from the downtown division evidence locker. The theft was attempted by two men, one of whom was captured, while the other escaped and is still at large. Circumstances suggest that the escaped thief masterminded the operation. His identity is at this time unknown.

The theft was clearly an inside job. The thieves had apparently been provided with a key to the evidence locker, as one was reported missing from the station. The missing key was later recovered after the escaped thief slipped it into the pocket of a five-year-old girl not far from the station.

The attempted theft was thwarted. Initial questioning of the captured accomplice has thus far proven unfruitful. He refuses to reveal anything, including the identity of his partner. He spends most of his time insisting he was tricked.

ଔଔଔ

December 8

ALL THAT SCHEMING, all that time spent—not to mention everything she had been forced to do—and it all almost went up in smoke. Literally. And then, after dealing with the problem, this attempted theft …

Amanda laid the police report and her notes side by side on the desk. If the thieves had succeeded in stealing that coded ledger from the evidence locker … she didn't even want to think about it. Instead she focused on the report. Two perps, and only one captured, while the other got away. And Amanda could not believe the identity of the one who'd been captured.

John did not wait for a response to his knock. Amanda barely had time to stash her notes in the drawer before John, hovering over her desk, tossed a sheet of paper onto the blotter.

"Thought you might like to see this," he said with a wink, "seeing as I've heard you mention the name before."

She glanced at the note. "Thanks, John."

He waited no longer for a dismissal than he had for an invitation to enter. Before Amanda could conjure a line of small talk, she found herself alone in the office once more.

She read over the note. Bryan West had been nosing around, asking questions about the Cahuenga arson and about Capaldi in general. Who had hired him to investigate? He could become a problem, if he got too close. He certainly had the brains to piece it together. Was Jonas on the trail, as well? That would be awkward, having to deal with Jonas.

After she had worked so hard, given up so much, she was not about to let it fall apart now. She was finally close to her goal, and she could not let them—or anyone else—ruin it. Her work on the Capaldi case—eight years of her life—was about to earn her a promotion. But if District Attorney Peyton knew what she had done to sew up the case, he would fire rather than promote her.

Of course, she could just as easily lose her job through personal indiscretion. Which is what made talking to Reeve such a gamble. But there was no choice: He was the only one who could help her. At least the conversation would take place up in the mountains, isolated from ears that mustn't hear what she had to say. And if he reacted badly, he would have time to cool off. He couldn't just run off and do something stupid. The reunion would give her a certain measure of control over the situation.

But she would be walking a thin wire. Bryan and Reeve were not the only threats. Who knew what Damien or Carter or Gideon—or any of the others, for that matter—had found out? The reunion would be the perfect opportunity to discover who knew what. And to find a way to make sure no one shared it with the wrong people.

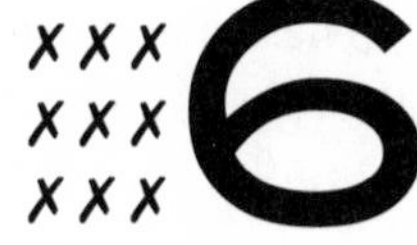

December 8

WHAT WAS HE going to do? Had he been fingered? Bennett sighed. The operation had quickly gone south, placing him in a pernicious double jeopardy. Not only would the police be looking for him, but Capaldi, as well. He would have to hide out here until Friday, not daring to venture out into civilization. The cabin had no telephone, television, or radio. He would be completely cut off from the outside world. But at least he would be safe. No one knew about the cabin.

So how had the stranger found him this morning?

He must have followed Bennett. But why? Clearly the stranger was connected with neither Capaldi nor the police, or Bennett would have been captured by now. In a way, that was even *more* troubling.

But not as troubling as the note Bennett had found in his mailbox yesterday morning. No address, no stamp. Hand delivered, not mailed. Which meant his location was not as secret as he had thought.

The note's contents had been disturbing, as well. Had it been a warning, or a threat? Who *was* in a position to know about his connection to Capaldi, or to piece it together? Gideon, of course. And Reeve Argyle. Amanda Farrell, the snoop. Perhaps Damien Anderson, and if so, possibly his brother Carter. Bennett was fairly certain he had seen Bryan West in the area, as well as Jill Constable. And of course Hatter Cates had been nearby. Virtually everyone from the Anderson Detective Agency. That's what the note was implying, wasn't it? That they were all in a position to stage a repeat performance of what they had done to him fifteen years ago.

Exactly as the visitor had pointed out this morning, reminding Bennett of their little prank with that actress, Dolores, fifteen years back. How had he known about that?

They had all tormented him, as he had been tormented since childhood. First by his own parents: "*Who put that idea in your head, Bennett? Eddie? Or was it Christopher this time?*" Then his elementary school classmates, pursuing him with relentless glee: "*Copycat! Copycat!*"

And now his good-for-nothing detective school classmates were in a position to do so much more than humiliate him. They could sabotage everything, as they had fifteen years ago. For it was they who had known him as Bennett Nash, before that name was replaced with a string of aliases; and that knowledge could lead the police—or Capaldi—straight to his doorstep. How much, exactly, did his former classmates know? There was only one way to find out.

That was where Bennett had outdone himself, deciding to use the reunion to learn what they knew, what they had worked out. How providential that the visitor should arrive this morning.

Something about the visitor had seemed vaguely familiar. A strange man. Studying Bennett's face, as if memorizing every line in it. Even going so far as to provide the clothes to be worn.

The stranger's plan was intriguing, if a bit crazy. A mystery none of them could solve.

Bennett wondered if he would have the nerve to go through with it. It was not as if he would have to worry about saying the wrong thing, after all.

What had the stranger called it? "A weekend of surprises."

And so it would be.

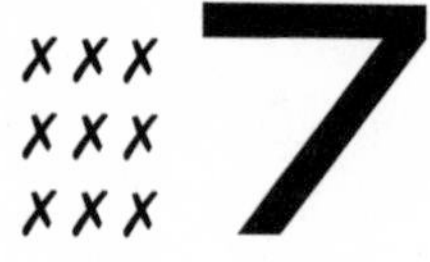

December 10

The Anderson Detective Agency cordially invites you to the fifteen-year reunion of your graduating class, which premieres at the train station in Owen's Reef, California, at 10:00 A.M. on Friday, December 12. I hope you will join the celebration at Moon's End, which will spotlight old friends, a few surprises, and perhaps even a little mystery to solve, if you still know how.

No RSVP.
Damien Anderson

GIDEON PUT DOWN the typewritten invitation and picked up the envelope. Los Angeles postmark. Sent to the diocese. No return address.

Perhaps Providence had placed Gideon in this motel, where Reeve was unlikely to find him. God works in mysterious ways, and maybe the bishop's wasting no time in evicting Gideon from diocese housing was one of them. Nothing is more embarrassing to the Church than a defrocked priest. Especially one defrocked for being a criminal.

He should have turned the rascal in. He probably would have, ultimately, if it hadn't been for that promise. *I'll help you find the culprit.*

A stream of images flowed through Gideon's head. A dark night, lights from a building. A noise. Walking toward the source. And then suddenly the ground falling out from beneath his feet … intense, blinding pain …

He bore them no ill will. It had not been their doing. It was not their fault that they were free to move about as they pleased, while he was trapped in this wheelchair. But to relive the moment in which he had gone from whole to half, a reminder of how unfairly G … Fate had dealt with him …

Who had been responsible for his accident? *He said he had evidence, in that uncanny voice he was using, and that he'd help me find who did it. That all would be revealed at the reunion. If I just stayed quiet.*

Well, what did he have to lose? Gideon asked himself. Squealing to the police wouldn't bring back his collar. Or his legs.

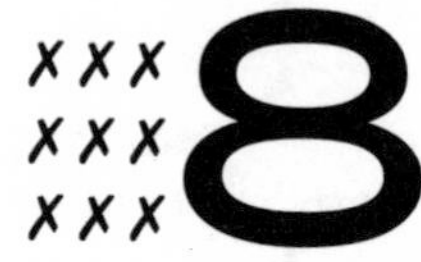

Transcript of a telephone conversation between
Antonio Capaldi and Jimmy the Switch*
(FBI Wiretap)

December 2

Capaldi:
It looks like I have need of your services.

Jimmy:
Of course, Mr. Capaldi. What can I do for you this time?

*Nickname of one of Capaldi's "cleanup men." Identity unknown.

Capaldi:
One of my men seems to have disappeared.

Jimmy:
With some of your money, I assume.

Capaldi:
No. It's a more … delicate matter. One requiring a certain discretion.

Jimmy:
Of course.

Capaldi:
A little over a week ago there was an unfortunate incident. A warehouse of mine was burned to the ground …

Jimmy:
And you think this guy—

Capaldi:
No. He didn't start the fire. However, an item was recovered from the fire … that shouldn't have been there. And I need to know how it got there. I also want to know why I haven't seen my bodyguard since the fire. Last time I saw him was the 24th—the day of the fire. That was over a week ago.

Jimmy:
And you're thinking—?

Capaldi:
I'm thinking he disappeared at the same time that a key appeared in my burned-down warehouse. And I don't like coincidences.

Jimmy:
And you want me to find him, right?

Capaldi:
His name is Reeve Argyle. I've sent over a photo and personal information. You should be receiving them within the hour.

Jimmy:
And when I find him, you want I should make your problem go away ... permanently?

Capaldi:
No. Bring him back. I have some questions I want to ask him.

Jimmy:
About the fire?

Capaldi:
About the key.

December 10

REEVE SAT IN the car, chomping on a cheeseburger and sucking down a chocolate shake. No beer: He had to keep his mind clear. This was the second day he was staking out Capaldi's mansion. So close to Capaldi, yet he was in no immediate danger. Capaldi would never suspect that Reeve would dare come this close.

Reeve never took his eyes off the mansion. And now his vigilance paid off, as he watched the figure disappear through Capaldi's gate across the street. Skulking like a cat. Jimmy the Switch. One of Capaldi's cleanup men.

So Reeve was right. Capaldi was after him. Reeve had known, when the hidden key disappeared—and then showed up after the fire—that he was in trouble. He was one of the few who knew where that key had been hidden; and if Capaldi blamed him for its disappearance, Reeve was a dead man. Especially now that the cops had Capaldi's ledger.

How *had* the thief—whoever he was—known about that key, let alone where to find it? And why steal the key, but not go after the ledger? And what was the key doing at the warehouse? Capaldi himself had personally arranged that fire; the people he had used could not possibly have known about the key or the ledger.

Somehow Reeve had to find out what had really happened and clear his name, before Capaldi found him.

Thank God Reeve had taken out that "insurance policy." He could not suppress a smile. Clever of him, and kind of ironic, too, when you thought about it: A church was the last place you'd expect to find Reeve Argyle.

Oh yes, he'd been clever. Like transferring all his mail to that post office box. He was expecting certain correspondence, to help him crack this thing, and he couldn't risk picking it up at his apartment.

He glanced down at the pile of letters on the front seat beside him. He picked up the envelope with the invitation and studied the post-mark: sent two days ago. Every year at this time, Damien vacationed at Moon's End for two weeks. He had already been up there a week, if he hadn't changed his habits.

This reunion would give Reeve a chance to disappear for a few days and plan his next move. No one would know where he was. For a while, he would be safe.

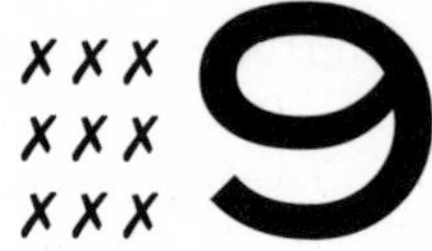

Eight Months Ago

INSPECTOR BUSH EXAMINED the bodies. Or at least the parts protruding from underneath the sofa. One male, one female. Both in their late teens. Crushed by the fall. Unfortunate, but not intentional.

So why had a homicide investigator been called to the scene of an accident?

"My men were hauling the sofa up to the eighth floor," the foreman explained. "These two kids were crossing under the ladder when the rope snapped. They never knew what hit 'em."

Bush frowned. "So why call Homicide? Looks like a cut-and-dried accident to me."

"You see that?" The foreman showed Bush the block and tackle.

"This is where the rope broke?"

The foreman nodded. "Notice the break: a clean cut, not frayed or unraveled. As if it were sliced with a knife."

Inspector Bush sighed. He would have to question all the curiosity-seekers, in case any were witnesses. How many were there? Eleven? Twelve?

Thirteen, counting the strange little man behind the crowd, in the gray homburg hat and green-and-gray tweed coat, taking notes on a notepad.

ଔଔଔ

December 11

Excerpt from Herb Kolander's review of
Beyond the Grave, *by Hatter Cates*

In Beyond the Grave, *Hatter Cates gives us another competently written but formulaic supernatural thriller. The plot is a variation of the time-honored Catesian theme of supernatural vengeance. Once again, a series of "disbelievers" are punished for their disbelief by the very supernatural forces they doubted, with gruesome but fitting deaths.*

On the plus side, Beyond the Grave, *like Cates' more recent offerings, benefits from a greater maturity of style. His early forays into the realm of the supernatural suffered from a lack of psychological realism. But over the last several years, we've seen a transformation in Cates' novels. Reading his last few, one feels that Cates was actually present when the novels' incidents occurred, recording everything: what it felt like, how people were affected, what they did and said.*

Unfortunately, this is not enough to raise Beyond the Grave*—or any of the recent Cates titles—from the grave of predictability. His latest offerings suffer from a typical Catesian lack of imagination. The deaths seem to be culled from newspaper headlines. In* Beyond the Grave, *a young couple, Erika and Felix, walk under a ladder and are crushed by a falling piano. Eight months ago a young couple strolling a downtown Los Angeles street were crushed by a falling sofa from a sabotaged rig. In Cates' previous novel,* Playing with Fire, *a family is burned to death* *when their house catches fire, after their fourteen-year-old daughter breaks a mirror. Ten months prior to that novel's release, the* L.A. Times *carried the story of a family that died in a house fire. Police found evidence of arson, along with a broken mirror. One is led to believe that Mr. Cates lacks the creativity to dream up his own violent deaths. Either that, or that he causes these real-life accidents himself, to obtain good plot lines.*

ര ര ര

THE HEADACHE WAS a solar flare incinerating the cold dark void bounded by his skull. It was a flash of ball lightning in a lifeless desert at midnight. A blast of summer from a charred brick oven in the kitchen of an Italian restaurant.

The study was dark, save for the glow of a Tiffany desk lamp beneath which lay the scattered headlines. Hatter, shrugging off his green-and-gray tweed coat, scanned the articles with a scowl. Nothing. Did anyone realize how difficult it is to dream up the accidents that peppered his novels? You can't just open up a newspaper and find one.

It was one indignity after another. First Luca insists that Hatter make his novels more "realistic"; the editor wanted to feel like he was there at the accidents as they occurred. And then, when Hatter figures out how to pull that off, Luca demands greater "originality": exotic deaths meted out in exotic locales, rather than the same recycled gimmicks. As if it were that easy.

As it happened, Hatter had already worked out the premise of his new novel: a gathering of people, destroyed one by one by the spirits of those in whose deaths they had played some part. But the plot details were stubbornly avoiding his mind's grasp.

And then the invitation arrives, a timely gift of Fate. For hadn't he intended to write about just such a gathering?

He would call it *The Final Reckoning* and use his former classmates as fodder. He savored with cruel anticipation all of the delicious mishaps that might transpire at the reunion.

For Hatter was certain that *something* was going to happen.

XXX XXX XXX 10

December 12

Gideon wheeled himself across the parking lot. Four of them were already gathered in front of the train station.

Bryan West had changed very little. Jonas Cruz looked older, but was still distinguished by his Latin good looks. The pretty blonde in the heavy overcoat had to be Jill Constable. But who was the tall, slender man? He resembled a grayer version of Carter Anderson, Damien's younger brother.

Gideon glanced around the nearly empty parking lot. *He's not here. He hasn't arrived yet.* Would he show up, or had that simply been a ruse to keep Gideon quiet? If so, it had only postponed the inevitable, for what was to stop Gideon from talking to the police when he returned from the weekend?

Reeve hadn't arrived yet, either. Would he? *Dear Lord, what am I afraid Reeve will do?* Gideon had been part of the solution; now he was part of the problem, a loose end. How would Reeve try to tie it up?

The others had far less trouble recognizing Gideon than he'd had identifying them. The wheelchair, of course.

"Gideon," Carter called. "I'm glad you came."

"We were just catching up," said Jill. "So what have you been up to since we graduated?"

"I became a priest."

"You're a priest?" Carter exclaimed.

Gideon squirmed. "Well, I'm thinking of taking a different position in the church. One with fewer responsibilities."

Jonas eyed Gideon. "Aren't you a bit young to retire?"

The cold northern California air seemed thin and hard to breathe.

11

There they were, before the train station. The man with the creased forehead sitting in the wheelchair could only be Gideon Lane. Gideon: He would know a lot, and Amanda fully intended to harvest that knowledge. Starting with the identity of the person behind the attempt to steal Capaldi's coded ledger from the LAPD evidence locker.

Jonas was fawning over Jill. Amanda could see him almost drooling. She tried to quell the traitorous lurch of her gut. Jill was her friend. Jill had never done anything to bait the hook Jonas had snapped at. Sure, there had been that one moment of weakness, but hadn't Amanda succumbed to one of her own?

The other two were not large enough to be Reeve. The shorter one had to be Bryan. But to whom was he talking? It looked like a prematurely aged Carter Anderson.

So Reeve hadn't arrived yet. Amanda had never been the nervous type, yet her stomach roiled at the thought of what she had to ask him. How would he react? If he knew what she had done to get a conviction against Capaldi, he would probably kill her. Not that she would blame him. Look at the dilemma she had created for him. She had even put his life in jeopardy.

"Amanda?" Carter asked as she approached. "Is that you?"

"Amanda Farrell," Gideon said. "What have you been doing these last fifteen years?"

"I'm a deputy district attorney for the city of Los Angeles."

Was it her imagination, or did Gideon shiver in his wheelchair?

When the thin mountain air began to make "catching up" seem more like a long-distance marathon, the two women used the lag in conversation as an excuse to steal off and speak privately.

"Reeve's not here yet," Jill told Amanda.

"So I see."

"Do you think he'll show up?"

"He has to."

Jill did not seem as certain. "Are you really going through with it?"

Amanda shrugged. "What choice do I have?"

"If you tell him, you'll put him in a position to ruin your career."

"What can I do? It's our only chance."

Of course, even Jill did not know how much more than that was at stake. Amanda had told no one—not even Jill—about her recent activities. What no one knew, no one could reveal.

And her goal at this reunion, among others, was to make sure no one knew.

12

Reeve breathed in the sharp, unpolluted smell of freedom. Hundreds of miles from Capaldi, far beyond his reach. Reeve should have been relieved to be up here, but one look at the group assembled in front of the train station—Bryan West, Jonas Cruz, Gideon Lane, Jill Constable, Carter Anderson, Amanda Farrell—revived bitter memories. Suddenly Reeve felt twelve again, a prisoner of his trashy old neighborhood.

The others caught sight of him across the parking lot. Not everyone seemed to recognize him. Gideon appeared to be avoiding Reeve's eyes, fidgeting in his wheelchair. What was *he* uneasy about? He was safe, protected by his priesthood. What was with everybody, anyway? Amanda was looking at him strangely.

"What's everyone staring at?" Reeve called out.

Carter was the first to respond. “Is that you, Reeve? I barely recognize you.” Reeve had been a big guy back at Anderson’s detective school fifteen years ago, but since then he had donned a coat of muscle over his large frame. “Did you become a weightlifter or something?”

“Bodyguard.”

“Who do you work for?” Jill asked. “Anyone famous?”

“Not really.” Last thing he was about to do was announce his connection to Capaldi.

“Maybe Amanda knows some of your clients,” Jonas suggested slyly.

Reeve turned to Amanda. “It’s been a while, Amanda,” he said coolly.

Amanda shot him a warning look but said only, “Yes.”

This had to be awkward for her. None of the others knew about him and Amanda. Even he wasn’t sure he knew what it had all been about. And the way Amanda kept shifting her weight from foot to foot made it clear that she wasn’t sure what to think, either.

XXX XXX XXX 13

The yellow taxi cab pulled into the train station's parking lot. Hatter could barely climb out of the back seat in his gray ankle-length raincoat. In trying to lug the two suitcases out of the cab, he bumped his head against the roof, dislodging his gray rain hat, which he quickly reset on his head.

"That'll be $94.00," the cab driver said.

Hatter hopped back into the cab in horror, leaving his luggage outside.

"Keep driving."

"What?"

"Drive around for a few minutes."

With a shrug, the driver complied. They circled the train station three times and returned to the lot.

"How much?" Hatter asked.

"$95.00."

Much better. Hatter paid the driver, who seemed happy to get his money and drive off.

The others had already arrived. Cautiously Hatter approached.

One of them—whose brown face had to be that of Jonas Cruz—glanced at the monogrammed suitcases Hatter had set down.

"L.C. ... Lawrence Cates," Jonas declared. "Hatter."

"Lawrence Cates" was Hatter's given name; but ever since fourth grade, his peers had called him "Hatter." Virtually everyone but his parents called him that. But it was his parents who had bought him the suitcases.

"Why did you tell the cab driver to keep driving?" asked Carter.

"The fare was $94.00," Hatter replied. The others stared at him, as if that were not explanation enough. "The digits add up to thirteen. An unlucky number."

"You know," said the short-haired redhead, whom Hatter recognized as Amanda Farrell, "I've actually read a couple of 'informational' tracts you wrote. As I recall, you argue that the victims of violent deaths linger in this world to exact retribution on those responsible for their deaths."

"You give lectures on that subject," Jonas added, "at psychic conventions. Right?"

"There are supernatural forces all around us," Hatter explained, "whose role is to punish offenders."

Gideon spoke up. "Hatter, I w—." He paused. "I am a Catholic priest. The Church considers the notion of ghosts to be heresy."

Hatter would have presented an argument to open Gideon's eyes—all of their eyes—had it not been for the arrival of the van.

14

The van, faded and rust-flecked, pulled up to the reunion party and stopped. Two men emerged. The driver, a fairly tall man with bland, clean-shaven features and a thin layer of short black hair, wore cowboy boots, a brown-checked shirt, and blue jeans. His companion was a much older man whose dull eyes were unlit by any sense of purpose. The driver spoke in a hoarse and raspy voice.

"You must be the reunion party." His smile seemed as out of place as the guests felt in the deserted parking lot of the abandoned train station. "I'm Bill. And this is Max. Damien Anderson sent us to bring you all to Moon's End."

Something about Bill—not the muffled croak of his voice nor the way he scanned the parking lot with those intense blue eyes, as if looking for someone—seemed peculiar to Bryan. Something hard to pinpoint, yet vaguely familiar …

Bryan noticed Jill giving the truck driver a similar searching look.

"Have we met before?" she finally asked Bill.

Bill fidgeted. "I doubt it, lady," he said in his hoarse voice, withdrawing a cigarette from a packet and fumbling in his pockets. "Anyone got a light?"

Bryan struck a match for him as a dilapidated sedan pulled into the lot. From it emerged a man toting a suitcase and wearing the same type of gray ankle-length raincoat and rain hat worn by Hatter. Though roughly the same height and weight as Bill, the newcomer's similarity to him ended there. Inert brown eyes and an aquiline nose were set in a pale face beneath bushy eyebrows; a brown moustache with full brown beard garnished a face framed by long sideburns.

"This is Aaron," Bill explained, "caretaker at Moon's End." Aaron, maintaining a jittery silence, removed his hat and unbuttoned his raincoat, revealing wavy brown hair, brown boots, and an unzipped tan-colored down jacket covering the powder-blue work shirt and white overalls of a workman. "Don't expect him to say much," Bill added. "He's mute, can't utter a sound. He can hear and understand anything you say, but he's not the most brilliant conversationalist."

Bill took a head count. "Looks like we're all here. We really should try to beat the rain—"

But it was too late, for they all felt cold drops of Morse code tap a warning on their heads. Heavy rain shaken from clouds like leaves in fall drove the reunion party into the temporary shelter of the abandoned station.

"This will mean more snow at Moon's End," Bill predicted darkly.

Part Two

✗✗✗✗✗✗✗✗✗✗

The Game

15

THE RIDE TO Moon's End was as dangerous as it was beautiful. The mountaintop slept beneath a blanket of fresh snow, trimmed with the silver lace of a treacherous winding road wet from the thickly dripping trees, for the snow here had given way to a long and heavy rain, scouring all but the sharp, pleasant scent of pine from the crisp and chilly air.

At length the road was rent by a cleft in the mountain stitched with one slender thread: a rickety wooden bridge spanning a deep ravine. The van jostled the waterlogged bridge as it crept across the chasm. More than one prayer was sent skyward as the passengers crossed, more than one sigh of relief heard upon their reaching the other side.

That side was a sparsely covered plateau, shrouded in snow, where the peak formed an isolated summit not more than one-half mile in any direction, linked to civilization solely by the bridge they had just crossed. Up here you could scream forever and no one would hear you.

The only flaws in the unbroken monotony of the freshly fallen snow were small stands of narrow-trunked rain-drenched trees and, at the center of the plateau where the road ended, a two-story inn: the legendary Moon's End. This was the first time any of them, except Carter, had seen Damien's prize acquisition. The nearest neighbor was at the base of the mountain across the bridge and down twenty-six miles of winding road.

The guests swarmed the inn, drawn by its mystique: the old-world grandeur of the balcony's walnut balustrade, the exotic window shutters and intricately carved exterior trim. Built long ago to lodge anticipated hordes of visitors, its inaccessibility had been its death sentence. Damien, in search of a winter retreat, had bought it a timely reprieve.

Something about the scene troubled Jonas. Unless Damien had arrived by taxi, his car should have been visible. But the building that served as a garage, a freestanding structure several yards from the inn with its door gaping, was empty; and because the road ended at Moon's End, Jonas doubted a vehicle would be discovered behind the inn or garage.

Eager to escape the cold, the former classmates lugged their suitcases through the unlocked front double door of the inn. Inside they found the same attention to detail they'd seen on the exterior: ornate carvings on the banister of the staircase descending toward them, a western-style hanging lamp suspended above the table in the parlor room on their left. But no trace of Damien.

The guests removed their coats, grateful to be inside, where their words were not etched on the frosty air in plumes of condensing steam.

It was Hatter who made the first significant discovery: a typed sheet of paper on the parlor room table, assigning rooms. And a set of labeled room keys.

Strange, Jonas thought. *Room assignments?* Why wasn't Damien here to escort them to their rooms in person?

Gideon observed that the antique style of the lodge had not prevented Damien from adding well-concealed electric wall heaters to Moon's End.

"The wood furnace in the basement stopped working," Carter explained. "Damien chose an updated heating system that wouldn't clash with the decor."

At length, the novelty of their surroundings could no longer distract them from the one unsettling issue.

"So where's Damien?"

"Outside?"

"There's nothing out there but snow and trees."

"Maybe he went home," Reeve suggested. "Perhaps this is all just a big joke."

Carter shook his head emphatically. "No. Damien always comes here for two weeks. The second week's not over yet."

Bill addressed Carter in his hoarse, guttural voice. "Your brother wanted me to tell you that if he wasn't here by supper, you should eat without him. There's plenty of food in the kitchen."

Enough for several days, in fact, the kitchen cabinets and refrigerator revealed.

"You're in Aaron's hands from here on," Bill concluded. "I'll be back to pick you up on Sunday. Say about noon."

With that, Bill returned with Max to the van and drove cautiously over the wooden bridge, which shuddered fearfully under the vehicle's weight. The van seemed to slow almost to a stop as it disappeared around a bend.

XXX XXX XXX 16

"So now what?" Reeve asked in the parlor room, casting fitful glances at the brown wallpaper depicting the deserted wooden buildings of a Wild West ghost town.

"I *knew* there was something fishy about that invitation," Hatter muttered. "Getting it at the last minute like that. Mine came just a day or two ago."

"Mine too," Jill said.

A general assent. They had all received invitations within the last two or three days.

"And isn't it more than a bit odd to be told *not* to RSVP?" Amanda asked.

"Damien must have sent the invitations from Owen's Reef, just before—or after—coming to Moon's End," Carter suggested. "No RSVP, because he wouldn't have answered the phone, anyway."

"I thought your brother came here to get *away* from everyone," Gideon objected.

"Well, there's nothing we can do about it now," Reeve said. "I'm going to my room." He consulted the room assignment chart. "Upstairs. Just past the staircase. Next to yours, Hatter."

Reeve chose a labeled room key from the table and studied it.

"Security keys," he observed. "Keys that can't be duplicated."

"The inn came with security locks," Carter explained. "The owners didn't want anyone duplicating the guests' room keys. Damien broke the master key in one of the locks and never bothered replacing it—not intending to entertain guests."

Suitcase in hand, Reeve lumbered toward the stairs. At the foot of the staircase, in the shadow of the bottom step, something on the floor arrested his progress.

"What is it?" Carter asked.

Reeve picked up the item and examined it. "A cigarette lighter."

"Damien must have dropped it," Jill suggested. "Guess he never gave up smoking."

"Yes he did," Carter replied, taking the lighter and studying it. "Years ago."

With a shrug, he turned to Aaron, who was casting restless glances at his wristwatch.

"Why don't you hold this until Damien arrives?" Carter placed the lighter in Aaron's outstretched left hand. Aaron dropped the cigarette lighter into the left front pocket of his white overalls.

After checking the room assignment chart, Amanda and Hatter followed Reeve toward the staircase. Gideon, glancing at the chart, guided his wheelchair toward the corridor leading off the parlor room to the downstairs bedrooms.

"I'd better go have a look around," Carter said. "Make sure everything's in order. With Damien gone, I guess that puts me charge."

Aaron peered one last time at the ornate timepiece on his right arm. A Rolex watch, Jonas noticed, inconsistent with Aaron's blue-collar garb. Furtively donning his jacket, Aaron stole a parting glance at the remaining guests—Bryan, Jill, and Jonas—before making a stealthy departure out the front door of the inn. Jonas wondered briefly what business could be taking Aaron outside.

"Well, I guess I'll leave you two alone," Jonas said awkwardly, grabbing his room key and valise before departing.

Bryan shifted his weight uncomfortably once he and Jill were alone. "Look, Jill, I—"

Jill looked away and shivered. "It's cold in here."

"What do you want from me? What do you want me to do?"

"I want back what you took from me."

"Every time I try to fix something, it just breaks something else."

Jill looked down. "I'm sorry about your sister. I really am."

Bryan fumbled with the leather cord around his neck. "I got down on my knees and begged Prissy's forgiveness. She had no idea what I was talking about, of course."

Jill said nothing.

"Does the wrong choice really make you a bad person?" Bryan continued. "At least I tried. I've kept my distance from you all these years."

"You kept your distance even when we were together."

When Jill left with her luggage and room key, Bryan consulted the room assignment chart. He noted his assigned room. Downstairs. Next to Jill's.

How was he going to survive the weekend?

17

It was very odd about Damien. Where had he gone? Carter was not the only one who so wondered, as he discovered when Jonas joined him in the kitchen.

"Carter, level with me," Jonas said. "*Do* you have any idea where Damien is?"

"You know Damien." Would Jonas accept that as an answer? Why was he concerned? After all, Damien could simply have driven down to Owen's Reef for supplies. But all the supplies they'd need were already here. Of course, Jonas didn't know that. Perhaps he was thinking about that cigarette lighter Reeve had found. Perhaps he realized what it meant: that they had not been the only visitors here.

Why did Damien have to make everything so difficult? Even when they were young. Carter had always assumed his destiny lay in accounting, as had Dad's. Until a series of poor decisions drove Dad's firm into the ground. Dad fell apart, relying on Mom's support. But while Carter felt abandoned and orphaned, Damien simply stepped into Dad's shoes. Damien had, after all, taken after their mother; it was Carter who seemed to have inherited so many of Dad's traits.

Then Damien established the detective agency, adopting Carter, taking him under his wing. Blazing the trail for Carter: like brother, like … No, that's not right.

None of them knew about Rodriguez. None would understand, if they did. To what does a man owe his loyalty? Family? His profession? Upholding justice, as Carter had sworn to do? Which one has the strongest claim?

The only answer to reach Carter's ears was a faint click, like the closing of the inn's front door. Peering from the kitchen through the billiard room, Carter caught a glimpse of Aaron making his way down the entry hall toward the stairs. The caretaker had come in from outside. His tan down jacket and white overalls appeared ruffled. What could he have been doing out there?

Carter heard the sound of Aaron's footfalls echoing up the staircase.

REEVE WAS OPENING the door to his room when Amanda appeared at the top of the stairs. She stopped before him.

"Reeve, we need to talk."

Reeve did not look at her. "Isn't it a little late for that? Six years too late?"

"Look, I get why you're mad at me. I do. And I don't blame you. What I did was wrong."

"Which part? The affair, or just walking out without a word?"

"Maybe both. It was complicated. If I could just explain—"

"What's to explain? I'm a bodyguard for a thug, and you're a high-class attorney—"

"I work for the city. That's hardly high class."

"You were raised in Beverly Hills. I was raised in a slum. Guys like me don't end up with broads like you."

"It had nothing to do with that, and you know it."

"Really? Then what did it have to do with?"

Amanda had never been good at masking exasperation. "Reeve, please don't make this harder than it has to be."

"For who, Amanda? Me or you?"

Before Amanda could make things worse by replying, Reeve disappeared into his room. Once inside, he took the gun from his suitcase. The gun his father had given him. Good old Dad, hammering his faded green punching bag—one, two, one two—especially, Mom said, on days Reeve was not around.

Detective work was exactly the chance Reeve had needed to escape from Dad's world. It had been easy to prove himself smart enough to enter a detective school. He'd had friends who could forge a high school diploma with no difficulty at all. Now he was a bodyguard for a powerful public figure, making better money than any of them.

Downstairs he had noticed a billiard table. Just what he needed to relax. He tossed the gun back into his suitcase, closed the lid, and opened the bedroom door.

Aaron appeared at the head of the staircase, out of breath. Now there was a bizarre one for you. Always avoiding your eyes, turning away nervously whenever you looked at him. For once, though, Aaron looked Reeve straight in the eye, unflinching. That was a first, this surprising newfound boldness.

Reeve descended the stairs and entered the billiard room. He was good at billiards. He considered himself good at many games.

Bryan laid the bed-pillow over the gun. Strange to think of a gun as a symbol of innocence. Yet he still recalled the excitement of purchasing his first handgun. A .357 Magnum, like the one buried under his pillow now. Innocence buried by time.

An eight-year-old boy might have felt rivalry toward his four-year-old sister, but not Bryan. He had always felt protective of Prissy. Which was why Mom, a psychiatric social worker, had felt comfortable leaving Prissy alone with Bryan when the emergency call came in that morning. Dad was at work with no time to make other arrangements, and it would only be for an hour.

It was in every newspaper in Los Angeles. The four-year-old daughter of Nathaniel West, district attorney of Los Angeles running for mayor, kidnapped two months before the election. Though half the LAPD was assigned to the case, Mom also hired a private investigator. Paul Templar.

Four days later Prissy was found. At first she seemed unharmed. But there must have been a struggle, for her head had struck something, damaging the prefrontal cortex. She was never the same after that. And it had all been Bryan's fault. She had been his responsibility.

But that was only the beginning. Under a counter in the abandoned tobacco shop where Prissy had been held hostage, police found Prissy's inhaler. Not only had the kidnappers known about Prissy's asthma, but they had also provided her medication. The police found this circumstance suggestive. They obtained a warrant to search the West family home. Bryan watched as they removed from a shoebox in Mom's closet a slice of the rope used to bind Prissy in the tobacco shop.

Every newspaper in the country carried the story. How Mom had staged the kidnapping of her own daughter two months before the election, to evoke sympathy for her husband. But with the scheme exposed, Bud Meynor, Dad's opponent, easily won.

Mom was acquitted; but Dad, never quite sure what to believe, could not bring himself to stay with her. The day he left was the last time Bryan ever saw him. Blaming Paul Templar for the loss of her husband and her daughter's cognitive impairment, Mom visited the detective with Dad's gun and came within an inch of blowing off his head. She died in prison two years later.

Dad, driven by guilt and shame deeper into the bottle, had miraculously remained sober enough to learn of his wife's fate. He followed her eighteen months later, with a drinking binge that culminated in a fatal car crash.

Four years after that, halfway through his seventeenth year, Bryan visited Paul Templar, for the sake of closure. Until Templar mentioned "the rope the police found in the shoebox in your mother's closet."

The media had indeed reported on the rope found in Mom's closet. But they had never mentioned the shoebox. The police had never released that detail. The only reason Bryan knew about it was that he had seen the police find it. And he had told no one.

So how did Paul Templar know about it?

That was when Bryan learned the truth. Bud Meynor's corrupt campaign manager, Marcus Bride, had orchestrated the kidnapping. And after Mom hired Paul Templar to find Prissy, Bride got to the private detective, offering him a huge payoff to obtain Prissy's inhaler and plant the rope in Mom's closet.

Unfortunately, Bryan could prove nothing. But if he could never see

Templar crushed under the wheels of Justice, there was still one thing Bryan could do.

He would become a private investigator. He would build up a clientele like Napoleon forging an empire, little by little, chipping away at the foundation of Templar's livelihood, until he drained the lifeblood from his rival's career. He would use any means at his disposal to crush his enemy.

Bryan smoothed the pillow covering his gun.

Any means at all.

18

Jonas hid the silver revolver in the dresser drawer. Strange: In his younger days he had never liked guns; his greatest weapon had always been his wits. He had never even held a firearm before becoming partners with Bryan.

For it was not violence, but childhood stories, that had first lured Jonas to the field of private investigation. Knights in armor, to begin with, then hardboiled detectives living exciting lives—but more important, living by their wits. Much more appealing than languishing on a farm, a skinny (thinner than brother Pedro), weak (weaker even than Raul) laborer, *as impressed with rhinestones as with real diamonds*, Papa had always charged.

Jonas felt the need for fresh air. Down the stairs, through the entry hall, past the sound of someone playing billiards.

The air outside was crisp as chilled lettuce. Jonas was not alone. The final flakes of a recent snowfall were frosting Bryan's hair.

Despite the breakup of their partnership, Jonas bore Bryan no ill will. Even during their stormiest phase, he had never told Bryan what he had done eight years ago.

"Prissy would love it up here," Bryan said without turning to face Jonas. "I saw her yesterday. Twice a week, like clockwork. She can never forgive me. She doesn't even know I did anything wrong."

"Did you ever consider the possibility that she might be right?"

Bryan turned around, his expression blank as the snow. "I vowed I'd avenge my family. Paul Templar and I cannot both stay in business. It's him or me." Bryan's body seemed to wilt. "Yet the more I try to untangle everything, the more tangled things become."

Jonas decided to risk an argument. "Which is exactly what will happen if you go through with your plan."

"Damien violated his oath to uphold justice when he started cooperating with Antonio Capaldi."

"And if you turn him in, you're condemning his brother, too. Carter works for him, and could very well go down with Damien as an accomplice. Even though he knows nothing about Damien's connection to Capaldi."

"Look, we've been through this all before. There's no point in refighting old battles."

"You know I have to tell Carter about his brother. I have to warn him about what you plan to do. It's only fair."

Bryan shrugged but said nothing. Bryan was right. There was no point in discussing it. Jonas breathed in the bracing air, savoring the dismal beauty. The sky was dark and overcast; the sun had not shown itself all day.

"Lovely out here," Jonas observed.

"Actually," Bryan said, "I was thinking about how isolated it is. In a way, we are not so much Damien's guests, as his prisoners."

ଔଔଔ

THAT WENT WELL, Amanda thought dryly.

She understood Reeve's anger. He would be angrier yet if he knew the full story. It wasn't easy working for District Attorney Peyton. How he demanded that all your energies be channeled to your job. Particularly if you were a woman. And if you were a woman hampered by the "distractions" of a husband or family, you could kiss goodbye any chance of grasping the ladder's top rung. Her only chance of achieving her ambitions was to provide herself with her own break, by cracking a high-profile case. Hence her investigation of Antonio Capaldi.

For nearly eight years she had been accumulating evidence against the mob chieftain with the patience of a bird storing seeds for the winter, one grain at a time, sacrificing countless off-duty hours to the career-making crusade. And when, two years into the investigation, she discovered that Reeve Argyle—her former detective-school classmate—was Capaldi's most trusted bodyguard, she crossed a line that had separated enthusiasm from ethics.

Getting close to Reeve had not been simply a backstage pass to Capaldi's secrets. It had been a tool, to be sure, but a tool wielded by a vulnerable hand to repair a splintered heart. Jonas had never been aware of her feelings for him, blinded by eyes that could see only Jill. There had been as much consolation as cunning in Amanda's seduction of Reeve.

Reeve had seemed to have genuine feelings for her. If he had realized the type of information he was letting slip, or what Amanda would do with it over the next six years, what would he have done? What would he do now? A wounded animal will behave unpredictably, and some arrows can pierce two targets at once, ego and heart. A double wound like that would be fatal to any hope she might have of enlisting Reeve's aid now.

She emerged from her room to find Aaron standing in front of Reeve's room, poised, as if having just come from it. What would he be doing in there? Even if Aaron's presence would not make a visit to

Reeve's room awkward, the timing was probably not the best. There would be time enough, after things settled down, to confront Reeve. Plenty of time.

ଔଔଔ

THINGS WERE WORKING out just as he had known they would. Hatter was not disappointed with his decision to come to Moon's End. He had known that something was going to happen, and the mysterious absence of Damien was a good start.

Hatter lifted his eyes to find Bryan and Jonas entering the parlor room. They must have come from outside, for he had heard the front door close.

"Keeping busy?" Jonas asked.

"Working on my new novel," Hatter replied.

"Are you the writer," Bryan asked, "or the ghost writer?"

Ghosts. Supernatural. Ha ha.

"I don't understand," Jonas said. "If you're so interested in the supernatural, why did you train as a detective?"

"I didn't always know what I wanted to do," Hatter replied.

Yet the seeds of his destiny had been planted in his youth, in the form of strange notions about the otherworldly and supernatural, the residue of bizarre science fiction stories by Hatter and his outcast teenage friends. These concepts earned their creators an unprecedented, if derisive, recognition by those schoolmates who had formerly paid them no heed whatever. But negative attention was better than none at all. Gradually time hardened controversial notions into a set of beliefs.

By the time Hatter graduated from Damien Anderson's detective training program, he had become so deeply rooted in the complex network of unorthodox beliefs he had helped to popularize, that to disentangle himself became decreasingly feasible. Their growth set the course of his life. Destiny deflected his path from private investigation toward a new goal: to champion, in fiction and on the lecture circuit, the cause of which he had suddenly found himself spokesman.

Hatter's entire adult career had been devoted to legitimizing all forms of superstition, but over the years his true passion gravitated toward the existence of deceased spirits lingering in the material plane to resolve unresolved issues.

"I read about that psychic fair in L.A. two weeks ago," Jonas was saying. "You were one of the speakers."

"Yes," Hatter replied cautiously. "I spoke about the influence of earthbound spirits on material existence. You're well informed."

"It's my job to know things. The article dwelt at some length on the tragedy that transpired outside the convention center. Apparently police were chasing an escaped criminal in front of the convention center. They believed he was drawing a weapon. A hot-headed young officer fired on him, accidently killing an innocent bystander in the crowd. The suspect got away."

Hatter shivered. He had heard about the shooting. He knew that the victim's spirit would not leave the earthly realm. It would haunt the material plane, seeking vengeance against all it held responsible for its death. But Hatter had been inside when the victim was shot. The spirit would probably go after the police officer who had fired the shot, perhaps the escaped criminal, and anyone else it felt had brought together the elements of its fate. Hatter had been only one of many speakers, although admittedly the keynote speaker. But surely he would not be singled out as the one who had drawn the victim to his destiny.

If he were, even the distance of hundreds of miles would not protect him from the ghostly hand of vengeance. But there was nothing to connect Hatter to a victim whose name he did not even know. He was safe.

19

HATTER HAD SEEMED eager to leave the parlor room. Not long afterwards, Bryan and Jonas noticed Aaron furtively stalking the downstairs corridor, retreating from the cluster of bedroom doors and entering the parlor room. Though previously his custom to avert his eyes, this time he glanced briefly into theirs as he passed, challenging them with the riddle of an enigmatic smile; and, right hand opening the front door of the inn, he stepped outside, the second time he had done so since their arrival. Bryan and Jonas exchanged quizzical glances.

"I think I'll go to my room," Bryan said, stifling a yawn. "And rest."

But as Bryan disappeared into the downstairs corridor, Jonas, barely registering the clinking of billiard balls as he stood near the entry hall, was unconvinced. He could tell from his ex-partner's restlessness that though Bryan was heading in the direction of his bedroom, he was not going there to sleep.

Jill lay on the bed face down, to stop the room from spinning. She had come here to sort out her feelings. Just looking at Bryan rekindled the heat, but was it the heat she had felt fifteen years ago, or the kind that consumes all affection?

With Bryan she had felt safe, protected. Even now she could still feel the beat of a heart swollen by desperate love, like waters swelling behind a dam, deep and enduring. If you love someone, you can never stop. But what if you can't forgive someone you can't stop loving?

What was she doing, wiping her tears on the pillowcase? If she had to go through with this, she would do so with dignity. With the aid of her compact mirror, she applied makeup below eyes that were sometimes warm lavender, sometimes cold cobalt, but always intense. She dragged a comb through her blonde hair, parted in the middle, recalling against her will Bryan's hand ruffling through it, with the encouraging praise of "Good girl."

On the end table beside the bed sat her bottle of clonazepam. She swallowed a pill, to calm her nerves. Slowly she unpacked. The walk-in clothes closet, thankfully, was spacious.

After Bryan, her love had drifted lost through the dark forest of her heart. Of course there had been no choice but to break up with him. His intentions may have been noble, but even the best intentions sometimes sprout toxic leaves. Perhaps she would tell Bryan about Jonas, to wound Bryan as he had wounded her. But once you set foot on the road to vengeance, she knew, there's no turning back. Was she really prepared to make that journey?

One thing she knew for sure. She wanted Imogen back. She wanted her daughter back.

When Gideon invited the knocker to enter the room, Bryan crept inside like a man entering a confession box. Clean-shaven boyish face, brown hair in bangs like a medieval monk's. His soft-spoken voice lacked its usual ironic edge.

"Gideon," Bryan began as he sat in the chair before the writing desk, "you're a priest ... " Gideon didn't correct him. "How does one find redemption?"

"Well, Bryan," Gideon said, "first you have to sin."

Gideon knew what Bryan was referring to. Fifteen years ago, training at Anderson's, Bryan had shared his motives for becoming a detective: the kidnapping of his kid sister, the deaths of his parents.

"Sometimes redemption is seeing that you're not guilty," Gideon continued. "I think what you've been chasing all these years may not be redemption, but forgiveness."

"You're saying I should forgive myself?"

"No," Gideon said. "You should know there's nothing to forgive yourself for."

Amanda stepped out of the shower and dried herself off. She slipped on a new dress and reached for her—

Where was her room key? She had placed it on the dresser. At least, she thought she had. She searched the room. Where could she have put it? Could someone—

She checked her bedroom door. Still locked. The window lock was pressed in, as well.

She must have set the key down somewhere without thinking. This reunion had her so preoccupied. How could she have—

The thought was lost to the shrill pierce of a chilling scream.

20

Bryan was out of his room and down the corridor before Jonas could leave the parlor room.

"What was that?"

"I don't know. It came from outside."

Without further talk, the two men left the parlor room to investigate. In the entry hall they encountered Reeve emerging from the billiard room, followed by Carter.

Outside the front door, not even a ghost stirred in the barren plateau of snow and trees. A fresh snow had covered all but one set of footprints. Jonas tracked them, followed by his companions, around Moon's End to the door of a stand-alone wooden shed several yards from the side of the inn. The men entered.

They took quick inventory of the shed's contents. Propped against the wall to their left was a shovel; on the opposite wall hung an extension ladder. Crates and tools cluttered the shed. Behind a workbench stood Aaron, dissecting a wooden board with a saw in his right hand.

"Did you hear anything?" Jonas asked. Aaron shook his head. The mute caretaker's loud sawing had apparently muted the sound of the scream, as well. "Has anyone come in here? Did you see anyone?" Again Aaron shook his head.

A fruitless encounter. Departing the shed, the investigators circled the inn in vain pursuit of the source of the mysterious cry, completing the circuit with the discovery of Amanda, Hatter, and Jill standing in front of the inn, with Gideon just emerging behind them.

"Did you find anyone?" Amanda asked.

Jonas shook his head. No one.

"There's no place to go," Gideon observed. "There's nothing out here but trees, with trunks too narrow to hide behind."

"As if whoever—or whatever—was responsible just vanished into thin air," Hatter pointed out darkly.

IT WAS THE booming voice of Reeve Argyle, echoing down the staircase, that drew everyone from their rooms like an early dinner gong.

"Where is it?" Reeve shouted.

"Where is what?" Carter asked, stepping into the corridor.

"My gun," Reeve bellowed. "Somebody took it from my suitcase."

In the startled hush, Bryan and Jonas raced to their rooms, spurred by the same misgiving. Jonas was the first to return.

"Mine is missing, too."

Bryan's eyes, as he reappeared, told the same tale.

"Did anyone else bring a gun?" Carter inquired.

No one had. Or at least no one admitted to it.

"Someone took those guns," Gideon said, glancing at the faces around him. "The question is, who?"

"No," Jonas countered. "The question is … why?"

21

Jonas summed up their plight with passionless efficiency. “A call for help that draws us all outside … then, suddenly, our guns disappear. It can't be a coincidence.”

“Someone lured us outside deliberately,” Carter suggested, “so that he, or she, could steal our weapons while the inn was empty.”

Reeve nodded. “The last time I saw my gun was before I left my room and went downstairs to the billiard room. That was a good forty minutes before we heard the scream.”

“And I was handling my own gun at roughly the same time,” Jonas corroborated. “Which confirms that the weapons were stolen sometime after that.”

In the awkward silence that followed, the front door creaked open. Aaron entered the parlor room and seated himself in an empty chair.

"So when did the thief enter Moon's End and take the guns?" Bryan asked.

Jonas thought for a moment. "I was in the parlor room when the scream came, so I would have seen anyone who came through the front door. You have to pass the parlor room when you cross the entry hall. You joined me shortly thereafter, Bryan. We encountered Reeve in the empty hallway coming out of the billiard room."

"I came from the kitchen, through the billiard room, before you were out the door," Carter reminded them.

"There's a door in the kitchen that leads outside," Jonas observed.

"Yes, there is," Carter replied. "But forget it, if you're thinking I made that racket outside and then ducked back in through the kitchen door. To get to the bedrooms—and the guns—from there, I'd have to have gone through the billiard room. But Reeve was in the billiard room and would have seen me. Which means I would have had to wait for Reeve to leave the room. That wouldn't have left me enough time to grab the guns, upstairs and down, and join you three in the entry hall before you were out the door. Besides, you would have seen me leave the billiard room."

"Maybe the thief didn't enter the inn through the front door," Amanda suggested, "but through the kitchen door."

"Impossible," Carter said. "That door was locked."

So the thief had entered through the front door; and, as no one had come through that door between the scream and the time the four men left the inn, the intruder had to have entered sometime after that.

"But before I got outside," Jill added. "I was the first one out after you four left. No one could have gotten past me through the front door without me seeing them."

"So whoever got inside," Carter said, "did so between the time we left and the time Jill arrived."

"If someone had gone up—or down—the stairs once I came out of the parlor room," Gideon reasoned, "I would have seen him. Which means he had already been upstairs and come down by the time I entered the entry hall."

"Unless," Jonas argued, "he robbed the downstairs first, went upstairs before you got out, and never came back down."

"You mean he left the inn from upstairs?" Reeve asked.

"Through a window," Hatter suggested.

"That should be easy enough to verify." Bryan and Jonas slipped outside and returned a moment later.

"Four of us circled the inn after the scream," Jonas explained, "but we never got near the inn itself. And there are no footprints now beneath any of the windows—first or second floor. So the thief couldn't have left through a window."

"Which also means that he did not *enter* Moon's End from any of the windows," Bryan added. "He did indeed enter through the front door."

So the intruder had not robbed the downstairs first, then gone upstairs and left the inn through a window. That meant he had robbed the upstairs first, then downstairs—but would not have had time to beat Jill to the front door. And after that, he couldn't have left through the front door without being seen by Jill. Nor had he departed through a window. Which left only one possibility.

"The door to the kitchen," Bryan said. "I noticed some footprints outside by it—"

"They were ours," Jonas countered. "I tried opening that door, but it was locked, like you said, Carter."

"Damien keeps it locked and bolted," Carter explained. "I never unlocked it."

A quick check confirmed Carter's claim. Bryan found the bolt drawn across the inside of the kitchen door.

"But," Bryan asked, "if the intruder departed through the kitchen door after Carter left the kitchen, how did he rebolt it *from the outside?*"

The answer, of course, was that he could not have.

"Yet if he did not leave through the kitchen door—or the windows, or the front door before or after Jill reached it—then he couldn't have left the inn at all."

"Which means he's still here."

Three groups searched the inn. Amanda, Reeve, and Carter

searched upstairs. Bryan and Aaron inspected the billiard room, dining room, and kitchen. Jill, Hatter, Gideon, and Jonas checked the drawing room, parlor room, library, and downstairs bedrooms.

But, aside from the eight guests and Aaron, the inn was as empty as a politician's promise. Bryan and Aaron examined the kitchen door for signs of tampering but found none. Hatter and Jonas uncovered behind the staircase a door beyond which a flight of stairs descended to the basement. There they found a collection of cobwebs and a non-working furnace, but no window, door, or other way out of the basement.

And no intruder.

Most of the guests reassembled in the parlor room to report what they had, or had not, found.

"We've searched every inch of this place. No one's here."

"But he couldn't have gotten out," Reeve protested. "We've already determined that."

Hatter shook his head. "What will it take to convince you people?"

"Don't start that nonsense again, Hatter. This is not one of your ghost novels."

"How else can you explain it? Someone took the guns. He couldn't possibly have gotten out. Yet he—and the guns—*are not here*. What other explanation is there?"

"How about," Bryan suggested, "that the guns were stolen by one of—"

But he never had a chance to complete the remark, because of the chilling scream from upstairs. Not from a mysterious source this time, but from Amanda.

All except the wheelchair-bound Gideon hastened to the second floor. At the top of the staircase they encountered Carter emerging from one of the bedrooms, in pursuit of the same sound. Like bloodhounds they tracked it around the corner of the upstairs hallway to the quivering figure of Amanda, covering her mouth with both hands. To her right, a closet huddled in the shadow of a wall's recess, its door swung open like a mouth hungry for a meal—or, in this case, having just disgorged one.

Stretched across the floor at Amanda's feet lay what might have been her shadow—had it been facing the right way. But it cut across the hallway widthwise rather than lengthwise, as if defying the light.

Carter was the first to reach the corpse. He turned it over gently and recoiled at the sight he had uncovered.

Rising from a patch of shirt sparsely daubed with blood in the center of the man's body was the hilt of a deeply-buried knife.

"It's Damien," Jill gasped.

XXX XXX XXX 22

Bryan examined the corpse. "Stabbed through the center of the upper abdomen. And the angle of the blade … slight upward trajectory …"

"From the position and angle of the knife," Jonas declared, "I think we can conclude that the blade sliced right through the aorta."

Bryan agreed. "A major artery. Near the surface of the skin."

With morbid interest Hatter examined the wound beneath the red-daubed shirt.

Jonas looked at Bryan, their professional instincts overriding their emotions. "How long would you say he's been dead?"

"At least since this morning."

Aaron arrived on the scene, staring at the corpse with an expression Bryan could not fathom.

Carter's voice struggled through strangling tendrils of shock woven across his throat. "We need to notify the police."

"Where's the telephone?" Jill asked.

Carter led them on a pilgrimage to the second-floor bedroom Damien always slept in. On a night table beside the bed sat the telephone Damien never used. Carter lifted the receiver to his ear. "Static."

Reeve snatched the telephone receiver and listened for himself. Static. He tried punching "0" on the keypad. Nothing. 911. Nothing.

"I knew the phone would be out," Carter said. "I couldn't get through when I tried calling Damien this week. My email bounced, too. The Internet must be down. The study is up here. That's where the computer is."

Carter headed for the study with the others at his heels—until Jonas veered down the stairs.

"Where are you going?" Hatter called.

"Outside."

Before anyone could ask why, Jonas disappeared down the staircase.

The others entered the study, where an outdated computer sat on a desk beside a dust-covered printer. Carter turned on the computer and tried to access the Internet. The monitor blinked, then displayed:

A SERVER CANNOT BE FOUND.
PLEASE CHECK ALL CONNECTIONS.

Anxiously the guests tested the cables between the computer and modem. All of the connections were solid. Carter tried once more to get onto the Internet, with the same results.

"Why can't we get anything?" Jill asked.

"Because," came Jonas' voice from the study door, "the phone line has been cut. That's why the phone is out. This computer's Internet service is routed through a modem—which is connected to the telephone line. No phone service, no Internet."

"Then we use our cell phones," Hatter declared, unholstering his own.

But his attempts to contact the outside world met only with frustration.

"I'm not getting a signal," he muttered.

"There's no cell phone reception up here," Carter explained. "You're wasting your time."

But Jonas, Bryan, and Amanda all produced their cell phones, with the same results.

"I told you," Carter said. "Cell phones are useless up here."

"Then we have no way of contacting the outside world?" Hatter asked.

"What's going on up there?" Gideon called from the foot of the staircase.

The others filed out of the study toward the head of the stairs. They apprised Gideon of their predicament.

"So we're stranded on a mountaintop with no transportation out," Gideon muttered.

"We're a good twenty-six miles from Owen's Reef. And it's all winding mountain road. Damien's car is gone. So we're stuck here until Sunday—unless anyone has a suggestion ..."

"I suggest we do something with Damien," Amanda said.

"Such as?" Carter asked. "The police will want his body for an autopsy. We have to preserve him as best as we can until then."

"I don't think we have to worry about that." Jonas glanced out the hallway window. "It's cold enough up here to preserve his body just fine as it is."

"You have a point, Jonas," Bryan agreed. "Medical examiners place corpses in deep freezers until they can perform an autopsy. And with the mountaintop covered in snow, we have our own personal freezer."

"Bury his body in the snow," Reeve suggested.

"Exactly. It will preserve his body—and the evidence—better than any other method."

The others gave their assent to Bryan's plan.

"It'll be dark soon," Hatter observed. "Let's get this over with."

Reeve, Bryan, Jonas, and Hatter carried the body outside. Aaron found a shovel in the indoor service porch off the kitchen. A makeshift funeral delivered Damien to his frozen grave.

Back inside the inn, the stealthy burglar Death robbed everyone of their appetites.

"We need to figure out *why*," Jill was saying. "Why would someone come all the way up here to murder Damien?"

"Maybe this was the revenge of some criminal he had helped put behind bars," Gideon suggested.

"It would certainly be the ideal place for a murder," Reeve added. "No witnesses."

"Aren't we just *assuming* it was murder?" Hatter's tone was almost patronizing. "How do we know it wasn't suicide?"

"A gruesome way to commit suicide. Stabbing oneself in the gut."

"But possible."

Bryan turned to Amanda. "How did you find the body?"

"I was searching for the man who took the guns, like everyone else, when I noticed the upstairs hall closet. I opened the door, and out fell … the body."

"So that rules out suicide," Bryan said. "Amanda found the closet door closed. If you go upstairs and check, you'll notice that the door has no inside handle. Which means that there's no way to close it from the inside. If Damien stabbed himself to death in the closet, how—after stepping inside—could he have closed the closet door?"

"He couldn't have," Reeve agreed. "Someone had to have closed the door after him."

"And whoever killed Damien was someone who knew he would find him up here."

"But why hide his body in the closet? If he didn't want it discovered, why not just bury it or take it with him? No one would ever have found it."

"Maybe the murderer *wanted* it found."

"Then why hide it in the first place?"

"Perhaps," Jonas suggested, "he did not want the body to be found *right away*."

"More important right now," Carter added, "is there some connection between this murder and the theft of our guns?"

At that moment a blast shook the inn like a cradle rocked to the beat of some demonic lullaby.

"What in God's name was that?"

Jonas and Bryan were the first ones out the front door, followed closely by the others.

A few vagabond flakes of snow fell upon them, as if nature were abandoning her attempt to bury them alive. From the chasm that separated the promontory from the rest of the mountain range, billows of black smoke rose as from a funeral pyre. The guests raced toward the smoldering abyss over the layer of newly fallen snow, to be stunned upon arrival by the sight they no longer saw.

"The bridge!" Jill cried. "It's gone!"

XXX XXX XXX 23

WITHOUT A WORD, Jonas and Bryan began searching the rim of the ravine.

"What are you looking for?" Carter asked.

"The detonator."

"What will that tell you?" Hatter snapped.

"Maybe nothing."

But that did not stop them from searching, nor Reeve and Carter from joining in. It was the latter who made the discovery.

"What's this?" From behind a large rock, uncovered and completely exposed, Carter produced a wooden box, powdered lightly with fresh snow. Jonas knelt beside Carter to inspect the box. Inside was an electric mechanism.

"A detonation device," Jonas mumbled. "Set in a wooden frame."

He studied it with a trained eye. "The frame is balsa wood, cheap and porous. The device itself is simple—crude, actually."

"If it's a detonator," Hatter challenged, "then why was it placed *here*, on the mountain, instead of secured to the bridge itself?"

"My guess is that whoever did this was taking no chances. He knew that vibrations could cause the device to malfunction. Remember how shaky the bridge was when we crossed it? That made it too unstable a support on which to mount the detonator."

"Whoever murdered Damien must also have set the charge," Amanda suggested. "He must have rigged the explosive after killing Damien."

"It's not hard to see a pattern," Jonas muttered. "The stolen guns. The murder of Damien. And now this."

Hatter twitched nervously. "We don't even have a working telephone to call for help."

Carter closed his eyes to think. "Wait. I seem to recall Damien keeping a short-wave radio up here, in case of emergencies. If we can find it, we may be able to call for help."

Jonas rose to leave, the detonator device still dangling from his hand.

"You're bringing that thing?" Reeve asked.

"I want to look at it more closely." Examining the wooden frame, Jonas quipped, "If nothing else, we can always use it for firewood. The frame is bone dry, so at least it will burn."

The party returned to the inn, across the fleecy blanket of snow, past rain-soaked trees. Gideon, waiting restlessly at the front door, was told about the bridge. He joined the others in a search for the short-wave radio.

Bryan and Jonas searched the downstairs bedrooms and library, but it was Carter who discovered the radio in an upstairs closet. Yet the light from an overhead lamp offered a dismal diagnosis: The front of the radio had been smashed in, rendering it inoperable.

Back in the parlor room, Jonas was the first to speak.

"It's beginning to make sense. All of this—the missing guns,

Damien's murder, the blowing up of the bridge—is the work of one person. The one who sent those invitations."

"So Damien didn't send them, after all," Jill said.

"That would explain a great deal," Gideon agreed. "We all noted that it's not like Damien, who comes here for solitude, to undermine it by inviting company. Because—apparently—he didn't."

Jonas looked at his ex-partner. "Back at the train station, you had mentioned something about the envelope your invitation came in. Something about the postmark."

"Yes, I had noticed an L.A. postmark on the envelope my invitation arrived in. We received the invitations about a week *after* Damien came up here. Which means that he had to have sent them from here—from Owen's Reef—as you yourself pointed out, Carter. That would have given the envelopes a northern California postmark." Bryan's eyes narrowed. "But Los Angeles is in *southern* California."

"Perhaps Damien came up here a few days later this year," Amanda suggested, "and sent the invitations before leaving L.A.?"

Carter shook his head. "No. He left the same time as always."

"I had thought of that, too," Bryan said. "Which is why I telephoned Damien's agency to ask about it. They confirmed that Damien had left several days *before* the invitations had been sent. Invitations—I should add—they knew nothing about."

So *that's* who called the agency several days ago, asking when Damien had left on his vacation, Carter thought.

"Two months ago our secretary fielded a call from someone asking questions about the detectives who had graduated in our class fifteen years ago." Carter kept his eyes on Bryan. "Was that you, also?"

"No."

Hatter interrupted. "So you're saying that whoever sent those invitations waited until Damien was up here—"

"And cut the telephone line, knowing that Damien—who never uses his phone or computer, anyway—would never notice."

"Ensuring that Damien could not be reached."

"And could therefore not deny having sent the invitations."

Amanda regarded Bryan with narrowed eyes. "If you knew Damien hadn't sent the invitations, why did *you* show up?"

"For one thing, I didn't *know* Damien hadn't sent them. Which is precisely why I *did* show up. I knew something was going on. And I wanted to find out what."

No point, Bryan thought, in bringing up the note. No one needed to know his other reason for coming up here.

Reeve settled heavily into a plush settee, preparing to puzzle out the mystery himself. At his right elbow he noticed something lying inconspicuously on the end table beneath an oriental lamp.

He had just discovered the First Note.

XXX XXX XXX 24

REEVE READ THE note aloud:

> "THE CAST IS NOW ASSEMBLED AND THE SCENE IS SET. YOU ARE ALL ABOUT TO PARTAKE IN A GAME OF NINE MAN'S MURDER.
>
> "YOU ALL FANCY YOURSELVES GREAT DETECTIVES. WELL, WE'LL SOON SEE JUST HOW GOOD YOU REALLY ARE. I HAVE DEVISED A LITTLE CHALLENGE FOR YOU, A SMALL TEST OF YOUR DEDUCTIVE ABILITIES. IT'S VERY SIMPLE. ALL YOU HAVE TO DO IS CATCH A MURDERER.

"WHO IS THE VICTIM, YOU MAY ASK? WHY, LADIES AND GENTLEMEN, YOU ARE THE VICTIMS. THE SCENARIO: ONE BY ONE YOU WILL ALL BE MURDERED. YOUR ONLY CHANCE OF SURVIVAL IS TO IDENTIFY THE MURDERER AND STOP HIM, OR HER, BEFORE YOU ARE ADDED TO THE LIST OF CASUALTIES. CONSIDER IT A BATTLE OF WITS, THE SKILLS OF A FEW WOULD-BE DETECTIVES AGAINST THE CUNNING OF A MASTER KILLER. YOUR TALENTS AGAINST MINE.

"THE WINNER WILL BE THE ONE WHO SURVIVES.

"It's unsigned," Reeve said dryly.

Each guest in turn dredged the note to bring up clues, but only one was found. The message had been typed on ordinary blank white stationery. Its author had not wished to provide a sample of his or her handwriting. Which implied that it might be recognized by the others.

"So one of us wants to kill the rest?" Jill asked.

"Or," Amanda suggested, "a third party has a grudge against *all* of us."

"Who?" Hatter asked. "We all have different professions. We live in different areas. Who would even *know* us all, let alone have a reason to kill each of us? What's the common denominator?"

"Damien," Gideon said. "We all apprenticed with him fifteen years ago."

"Gideon's right," Carter agreed. "We used to help Damien on his cases, as part of our training. Investigating, doing research, writing up reports. Maybe we helped convict someone he proved guilty of a crime."

"And the convict blames us," Reeve added, "as well as Damien."

Jill nodded. "It makes sense. He killed Damien. Now he's after us."

Gideon swept an eye over the others. "We all trained as detectives. Perhaps there's something more we can infer from the note."

"Tone?" Jonas asked.

"Angry," replied Carter.

"Hostile."

"Taunting."

"Damien made no secret of his winter retreats," Jill said. "Everyone who knew Damien knows about them. So anyone could have used that knowledge to forge those invitations and lure us up here."

"Whoever *did* type this note," Jonas added, "had this whole thing planned out well in advance. Every stage seems to be under perfect control."

Amanda pondered. "All we really need to know is who put that note on the table, and then we'll know who wrote it."

"What if it was placed there before we arrived?"

Jonas shot down the notion with a shake of his head. "I was in the parlor room earlier this afternoon. That note was definitely not on the table at that time. Someone planted it there between then and now."

"Perhaps you put it there yourself," Hatter suggested, "when you were alone."

"All of us have had ample opportunity to plant it during the last two hours," Bryan said.

"Not to mention an outsider," Reeve added. "There were times when anyone could have come inside undetected."

"The mysterious outsider," Hatter muttered with his sandpaper chuckle. "The one who took the guns."

"The one we're trapped up here with," Jill pointed out soberly.

XXX
XXX
XXX

25

THEY DIVIDED INTO two groups. Bryan, Carter, Reeve, and Amanda scoured the promontory to sweep out the intruder, if there was one, with what little daylight remained. A large broom was not needed, for the mountaintop was no more than a half-mile square, bordered by a sheer drop of cliff on all four sides, with no shelter other than the narrow trunks of trees dappling the mountain peak. If someone was hiding anywhere on the summit, he would not be difficult to find.

Jonas, Jill, Gideon, Hatter, and Aaron searched the inn. Jonas and Jill ransacked the work shed and empty garage, finding no one. Circling Moon's End, the pair was stopped behind the inn by Jonas catching sight of something to the left of Bryan's window.

"What is it?" Jill asked.

"You see that trellis?" Jonas replied.

Stretching between Bryan's first-floor window and Amanda's

second-floor window was a white wooden ivy-twined square lattice-work, like others affixed to the walls of Moon's End—the one outside the kitchen and Reeve's room, for example.

"What about it?" Jill asked.

"Look at those two slats near the bottom. They're broken. I didn't notice that when we were searching for the source of that scream."

They completed the circuit of Moon's End, finding no footprints in the snow. Thus no one had evaded discovery simply by staying one step ahead of them.

A search of the inn yielded similar results. Not one inch of Moon's End was granted modesty or went untouched by human eyes, not even the cellar Hatter and Jonas had discovered earlier that day. The walls, ceiling, and floors of the inn concealed no secret compartments or passages in which a fugitive could hide. The only guests at Moon's End were those who had been invited. Nor did the search of Moon's End uncover any of the missing handguns. The only treasure the inn would yield was an old cassette tape recorder, still functional despite its years, with a tape of Damien's old dictation.

The outdoor party returned from their fruitless hunt.

"No trace of anyone out there," Carter declared. "And there's nowhere to hide."

"If anyone else is with us here on the mountain," Reeve added, "he's buried himself in the snow."

"There's no one hiding *inside* the inn, either," said Hatter.

Gideon's words mirrored the thoughts of the group. "That means that the person who wrote that note—"

"*Is one of us*," Jill finished for him.

"On the positive side," Amanda said, "the murderer is outnumbered."

"That won't stop him," Hatter promised.

"This is dreadful," Jill whimpered. "What are we going to do?"

"We're going to keep our eyes on one another." Was Carter trying to bolster Jill's spirits, or his own? "Mandy is right. It's seven against one—eight, including Aaron. And it's only for three days. When Bill and Max return for us on Sunday, they'll find the bridge out and send for help. If we all keep alert, nothing more can happen this weekend."

It was not the last time that weekend someone would be wrong.

XXX XXX XXX 26

THE FIRST MURDER—after Damien's—took everyone by surprise.

"We'll all think a lot better after we've eaten," Carter suggested. "I've got dinner working in the kitchen. I'll call you when it's ready." He disappeared into the kitchen.

What now? Carter wondered. *What would Damien do, if he had not gone where you can't follow, his death the ultimate abandonment?*

"Have a moment?"

The words startled Carter. He turned to face Jonas standing in the kitchen doorway.

"This may not be the best time to bring this up," Jonas said, "but I thought you should know. I don't know what Bryan plans to do, now that Damien's … gone. But there's something about Damien you need to know."

"You mean his business relations with Antonio Capaldi?"

Jonas' jaw dropped. "You know?"

"I found out. A little over two months ago an FBI agent named Rodriguez approached me privately. Asking me questions. Trying to determine if I knew about Damien's connection to Capaldi. When he was satisfied that I didn't, he told me all about it. He wanted my cooperation in building a case against Damien."

"What did you tell him?"

"What could I tell him? Damien's my brother. There's such a thing as family loyalty." Carter looked away. "Not that Damien ever subscribed to it." Carter moved from pot to pot. "What did I tell Rodriguez? I told him I'd think about it. Not that it matters now."

A noise turned both of their heads toward the kitchen doorway in time to see Reeve retreating through the billiard room.

JONAS FOUND REEVE in the drawing room. How much of his conversation with Carter had Reeve overheard? Better to confront Reeve later, in private.

Bryan had drifted to a corner of the drawing room and was staring blankly out the window.

"I've seen that look before," Jonas said. "Something's wrong. And it's not just Damien's murder."

With a dismissive sweep of the hand, Bryan drew the bolt across the door to his thoughts.

"Come on," Jonas urged. "I know when something's bothering you."

Bryan's resistance budged. "It's that note. Something about it is familiar, but I can't say why."

"Go on."

"It refers to the reunion as a game of 'Nine Man's Murder.' I can't help feeling that should mean something."

"I was puzzled by that, too. For one thing, there are only eight of us."

"Nine, counting Aaron."

"But the note made a point of us being detectives. That would let Aaron out."

"Actually," Bryan corrected, "we were referred to as 'would-be' detectives. Which in itself is a strange term to use. Some of us are licensed investigators. The term might have been appropriate fifteen years ago, when we were apprenticing with Damien. But not today."

Gideon, overhearing the conversation, wheeled himself into it. "Perhaps it's a play on words."

"How's that?"

"The name of the game. 'Nine Man's Murder.' Maybe it's a play on 'Nine Man Morris.'" This illumination left the shadows intact. "It's some kind of game," Gideon explained. "I don't know how it's played."

"It's a British board game, I believe," interjected Jill as she entered the drawing room. "I'm not familiar with the rules."

"I hate games," muttered Reeve, sitting nearby.

Bryan shook his head. "Somehow I can't see all this revolving around some English board game."

Bryan lapsed into a contagious silence, which infected all of the guests. It was cured by Carter's entrance into the parlor room, announcing that supper was ready.

In the dining room, all were greeted by platters of questionable-looking sirloin, green beans, and mashed potatoes basted in a lightly charred smell. Aaron helped his fellow mountaintop prisoners set the table, and, with the self-consciousness of a servant mingling with the guests, accepted an invitation to join them for dinner.

Not until halfway through the meal did a remark of Hatter's charge the leaden atmosphere.

"We're all going to die."

Bryan glanced up from his plate. "The food's not that bad."

"Shut up, Cates," Reeve ordered.

Carter's patience had been fraying since the discovery of his brother's body; now it began to unravel. "That's enough. We already have plenty to worry about without bickering."

But Hatter's nerves were as brittle as dried brush waiting for a wildfire. And Carter had just provided the spark.

"And who put *you* in charge, Carter? Now that your brother is out of the way, you figure you'll just hop into the helm, is that it?"

"That's enough, Hatter," Jonas snapped.

"For years you've waited to take his place," Hatter persisted. "You were jealous of him. You've always been overshadowed by Damien, first when you apprenticed with us, and then afterwards when you went to work for him—not as a partner, but as a mere employee."

Everyone expected Carter to launch a brutal counterattack. No one expected him to choose the weapon of placid tranquility.

"Let's say you're right," he reasoned softly. "After all, it *is* true that Damien ran the show. He never gave me a chance to prove what I could do." An introspective pause. "Jealous? That's a bit strong. But I *have* wanted to show what I can do on my own."

"So you came here early this morning to have it out with Damien," Hatter theorized, "before any of us. Just the two of you. You both fought. And you killed him."

"And if I knew that Damien was dead, why did I bother showing up for the reunion?"

"How would it look if you didn't? You would be the only one *not* to show up, because you were the only one who knew there would be no reunion, with Damien dead. But how would you know he was dead, unless *you* were the one who killed him? Not showing up would be as good as a confession."

"Cut it out, you two," Gideon pleaded. "This is exactly what someone wants us to do: argue with one another. The murderer wants to divide us, to make us more vulnerable."

But Reeve ignored Gideon's plea. "Of course," he said to Carter, "you could have been arguing with Damien about something else—"

"Reeve ..." Jonas warned.

"You could have been fighting about his business dealings with Antonio Capaldi."

Bryan dropped his fork on the plate. "How did you—"

"Damien was working for Capaldi?" Amanda gasped.

"And Carter here was going to help the FBI catch him," Reeve explained.

"But why kill the rest of us?" Gideon asked.

"To protect the sting," Reeve suggested. "Carter might have feared that some of us were getting close to discovering the truth and could reveal it to Damien, if we stumbled onto it."

"So Carter brought us up here," Jill said, "under the pretext of a reunion."

"But with Damien dead," Gideon pointed out, "there's no need to silence us. Carter no longer has a reason to kill the rest of us."

"Unless," Amanda countered, "*he's* not the one who murdered Damien. Despite any sibling rivalry issues, Carter loved his brother." Amanda addressed Carter. "You weren't counting on someone killing Damien. And you don't know who it was. Which gives you the motive of—"

"Revenge," Carter said.

It was not anger fueling the flames of Carter's flushing cheeks; nor was it the hand leaping to his throat that choked the words in his mouth, leaving only a faint gurgle. The fire in his face ripened from crimson to maroon, fanning through his body as Carter fell stiffly from his chair to the floor.

Several of the men rushed to Carter's side. Jonas, kneeling beside the prostrate body, touched two fingers lightly to the side of Carter's neck. His fingers groped for a pulse.

"He's dead," Jonas declared.

27

AMANDA, WITH HER reflexive skepticism, knelt beside the body to expose the hoax. But Carter's prank was so convincing, it had fooled Death itself.

"He's dead, all right," Bryan confirmed after Amanda.

"Poisoned?" Jonas ventured.

Jill pushed her plate away.

Reeve stared at the corpse. "His lips are blue."

"Cyanide?" Bryan asked Jonas.

"*He* prepared the meal," Gideon observed. "So how did his food get tampered with?"

"He might have taken something while he was alone in the kitchen," Reeve suggested.

"You mean, killed himself?"

"It must be. After all, we all ate the same food."

"Unless someone poisoned Carter's meal specifically."

Bryan looked around. "Did anyone actually *see* someone touch Carter's plate?"

No one had. The guests had set the table with preoccupied, and thus inattentive, minds. So, if Carter's meal had indeed been poisoned, anyone could have been responsible.

Jill's ear was caught by the sound she realized she should have been hearing, but wasn't. One might have expected this turn of events to be fodder for Hatter's obsessive harping on his favorite theme. While all eyes were on Carter's lifeless body, Jill glanced behind.

"Are you all right, Lawrence?" she asked.

The others turned in time to see Hatter, pale and glazy-eyed, double over, as if bowing from his chair, while clutching his stomach. His head hit the table with a thud.

"Is he dead?" Gideon asked.

As if in answer, Hatter moaned.

"Let me see him." Jonas pushed roughly toward Hatter. "Whatever he was given, I don't think he's had a fatal dose—or he'd be dead by now, like Carter. Here. Drink this." Jonas encouraged Hatter to drink water from a glass.

"Shouldn't we try to make him throw up?" Reeve asked.

"No!" Jill cried. "Not yet. It could damage his esophagus, or alimentary canal. Besides, he's barely conscious. He could end up choking to death on his own—"

"What are you, a doctor?" Reeve asked.

"A home health care provider, actually."

Jonas looked up at Jill. "See if you can find some milk in the kitchen."

Jill disappeared through the doorway.

"In the meantime," Jonas continued, "let's get him into the drawing room. We can lay him down on the sofa."

"What about *him*?" Reeve nodded at Carter.

"There's nothing we can do for him now. All we can do is take him outside and bury him in the snow with his brother."

Jonas and Amanda deposited Hatter on the drawing room sofa, while Gideon fetched a blanket from a linen closet to swaddle Hatter's remaining warmth. Bryan, Reeve, and Aaron conducted Carter's body outside to bury in the snow. It was the second corpse they had laid to rest in less than twenty-four hours.

It was not to be the last.

28

"HE COULD HAVE killed us all," Jonas was saying. "Simply by poisoning all the food."

The guests were assembled in the drawing room, their conversation punctuated by an occasional low moan from Hatter.

"So that's obviously not the killer's plan," Jonas continued, pacing before the fireplace. "Since he only tried to poison Carter and Hatter."

"And failed, in Hatter's case," Reeve pointed out.

"Yes, that's a significant point," Gideon added. "It's the first time the murderer has slipped up."

But Bryan did not look convinced. "If it *was* a slip-up."

All efforts to persuade Bryan to turn up whatever card he had in the hole were futile, and Jonas knew Bryan would not play that card until he was ready.

"Search everyone," Gideon suggested. "There's a chance we might find our man with the poison still on him."

Bryan shook his head. "This killer is no fool. He's had ample opportunity to get rid of the evidence. You won't find poison on any of us."

"You've been watching too many movies," Reeve said. "Just give *me* fifteen minutes with each of you, and I'll get a confession from the culprit."

"And from six innocent suspects. No," Bryan said darkly, "I think we're going to have to wait him out."

Reeve, with the sullen silence of a chastised child, receded further into the sofa. Silence tightened its grip on the room like a tourniquet, until loosened by Jonas.

"That's it!" he exclaimed, slapping his thigh. "Movies." The word was directed at Reeve, whose face remained blank. "You told Gideon he had been watching too many movies. *Nine Man Morris* was the name of the movie. Our graduation assignment. When we apprenticed with Damien."

"The movie set—"

"You mean the string of accidents we had been sent to investigate?"

"But that was fifteen years ago."

"You're right," Amanda said. "*Nine Man Morris* was the name of the film they were shooting."

"But that was where—"

All eyes darted to Gideon.

"What could all this have to do with some assignment we undertook as novice detectives fifteen years ago?" Jill asked.

Gideon fingered the facts like pieces of a puzzle. "Remember how the note was phrased? We were being challenged as *detectives*. And that assignment on the movie set was like our final exam. It was immediately afterwards that we graduated as fully credentialed investigators."

"Not *all* of us," Bryan said, looking at Aaron.

Silence.

"Bennett Nash," Amanda finally murmured.

"The only one who didn't graduate."

"I'd forgotten all about him," Jonas said.

"You know, it's strange," Reeve added. "The fact that we were all invited to this reunion, and he wasn't."

"Wasn't he?" The question had come from Bryan. "What do you think, Aaron?"

Whatever secret Bryan was trying to extract from Aaron, the latter would concede nothing but an inscrutable grin. The situation proved more intense for Jill, who sat opposite an end table from Aaron. She was mirroring his watchful scrutiny of Bryan, and with eyes thus engaged, her hand groped blindly for a glass of red wine she had set on the table. The inevitable collision struck down the unsuspecting glass, which bled across the table onto the leg of Aaron's white overalls.

"Oh, I'm so sorry," Jill exclaimed, springing from her seat. "Let me get something to wipe it up with, before the stain dries."

Then Aaron did something that, with one exception, astounded everyone in the room.

He spoke.

"That's all right," he said with a dismissive sweep of the right hand. "Don't bother."

"You can talk!" Jill gasped.

Bryan looked impassively on the face of this miraculous healing.

"I *thought* you were a man of too few words, Aaron … or should I say, Bennett?"

"HOW DID YOU know?" Bennett, abandoning his masquerade as "Aaron," asked Bryan.

"That you were really Bennett Nash? It's my job to know things." A favorite quote of Bryan's from the old days. "Something about you was familiar, though I must say you've changed a great deal over the years."

"I would never have recognized you," Jill agreed.

Indeed, a full head of hair had overgrown Bennett's formerly crew-cutted skull, while a moustache and beard had matured his once-boyish face.

"But there were two other points, as well," Bryan continued. "First, that scream we heard outside, which drew us all from the inn. We found no one out there but you. Of course, you were supposedly mute, which disqualified you as its source. The problem was, none of us could have gone outside to make that noise and then returned to the inn undetected—except Carter, and he appears to have been ruled out. And, as we later discovered, we are the only ones on this mountaintop. Which meant there was only one person who could possibly have been responsible for the scream. You. Hence, your muteness was a fabrication.

"Second, the disappearing guns. We were all working under the assumption that the purpose of that scream had been to draw us from the inn, leaving the weapons unprotected. We had all assumed that *that* was when the guns had been taken. But we later determined that it was impossible for anyone to have removed them at that time. Therefore, I concluded, that was not when the weapons had been stolen—which meant they had to have been taken earlier."

Bennett's eyes neither confirmed nor denied, offering merely a grudging appreciation of Bryan's reasoning.

"I remembered that several of us had observed you skulking around the inn earlier," Bryan continued, "just prior to your second departure from Moon's End. I don't know where you went the first time, but the second time, you entered the work shed." Bryan had spoken no more than the first half of his final sentence when the light of composure in Bennett's eyes, for once, seemed briefly to flicker.

"I think what you had been doing—before departing the inn the second time—was collecting everyone's guns. Then, later, to give yourself an alibi, you created the diversion of the scream to draw us from the inn and make us *think* the weapons had disappeared then—at a time when you could not possibly have taken them, because you were in the shed."

"All right, I suppose it's time for me to come clean," Bennett said. "A few days ago I received a telephone call from Damien—or at least someone claiming to be Damien. After fifteen years, I could hardly be expected to recognize his voice."

"That makes sense," Jill said. "If Bryan hadn't just told us who you are, I would never have deduced it from your voice." Although, Jill thought, there *was* something familiar about that voice.

Bennett glossed over the interruption. "Damien—or the person purporting to be Damien—told me about the reunion. I told him I wasn't interested. I had no desire to see any of you again—not after the ac— the way you had all treated me. The ridicule … The mockery … But he kept trying to persuade me. He told me he wanted to play a practical joke on all of you, and he needed my help. We would create a mystery none of you could solve—the disappearance of the guns—to remind you that he was still the best, still our teacher. It sounded kind of childish to me, and I told him so.

"But then he reminded me of how you all used to tease me, calling me a human Xerox machine, incapable of an original thought." A cold fire sparked momentary silver in Bennett's eyes. "I told him I would do it. That's when he explained to me the masquerade as Aaron." Bennett turned to Bryan. "You were right about the diversion—the scream. Its purpose was to mislead you as to the time the guns were taken. Because I was pretending to be mute, my role as the source of the scream would go unsuspected. You would all be looking for someone who had called you outside in order to gain access to the guns. None of you would be able to explain how the guns had disappeared. When the truth was finally revealed, you would all look like fools."

The speech was delivered as if rehearsed.

Reeve was watching Bennett with unveiled suspicion. "You say you thought it was Damien who had arranged all of this with you?"

"Over the phone. Yes."

"Surely, once we discovered Damien's body, you must have realized the truth. Yet you kept up the charade."

"Once the body was found, I was afraid to reveal myself. For fear of how it would look."

"And after you took the guns," Jonas asked impatiently, "what did you do with them?"

"I did what I had been told to do. I hid them."

"Where?"

"Down in the basement. In the old furnace."

Moments later Bryan and Jonas were bounding down the basement staircase, with Bennett and Reeve close behind. Carter had mentioned that the furnace no longer worked; it was, therefore, the ideal place in which to hide the guns.

Jonas' hand reached into the furnace but came out empty. The guns were gone.

"THEN I PLAYED right into his hands," Bennett said. "He used me to get to the guns, and I obliged him."

The guests had returned to the drawing room, on time to witness Hatter's shaky recovery.

"Well, at least we've established one thing for certain," Amanda said, branding each male guest with an accusing glare. "Our killer is a man."

"What makes you so sure?" Jill asked.

Amanda addressed Bennett. "You told us yourself. You said it was a *man* who called you, pretending to be Damien."

"You know better than that," Jonas told Amanda. "A woman could have gotten a man to make the call for her."

"I don't suppose you'd recognize the voice?" Reeve asked Bennett.

Bennett extended his hands helplessly. Looking at Bennett's face, Jonas noticed its lifeless, inexpressive quality. The strain of having pretended to be Aaron, Jonas decided.

"Ohh …" Hatter groaned like a maimed horse, attempting to lift himself into a sitting position.

"Are you all right?" Gideon asked.

"I'm fine, I think," Hatter said unconvincingly. He surveyed the room. "Where's Carter? Is he—"

"He's dead," Amanda replied.

"And you were lucky," Gideon said.

"From now on," Jonas advised, "we must avoid any food that could have been tampered with. I checked the kitchen, and luckily there's plenty of canned food."

"And everyone should prepare their own meals," Bennett added.

"You talk!" Hatter exclaimed.

"A long story." Jonas and the others chronicled Bennett's masquerade as the mute caretaker.

Bryan turned to Bennett. "You know, in light of recent developments, that cigarette lighter Carter gave you might be significant. Let me see it."

Bennett stared at him blankly.

"The one Reeve found on the floor when we first arrived. You put it in your pocket, remember?"

"Oh," Bennett said dully. "I forgot all about it." His hand burrowed into the right front pocket of his wine-stained overalls but emerged with nothing. The other pockets yielded the same.

"I … I don't seem to have it," Bennett stammered. "I must have lost it."

"Or it was stolen," Jonas suggested. "If that lighter was dropped by the killer when he murdered Damien, it might provide a clue to his identity."

"Which of us smokes?" Bryan asked the assembly.

"I quit a month ago," Reeve said.

"You smoke, Bryan," Amanda said. "I saw you offer a match to that truck driver, Bill, who brought us here. A match—not a lighter. Had you lost yours?"

Reeve swept an accusing eye over Bennett. "Or Bennett is lying about not having that lighter."

Bennett looked amused. "You're welcome to search," he said.

Reeve frisked Bennett hastily and found nothing.

"Of course," Bryan said, "the lighter may mean nothing at all. It may have been a plant. A red herring. Left intentionally by the murderer to incriminate someone."

The fire in Reeve's red face nearly scorched his onlookers.

"You mean like …" Gideon began.

"The ring," said Amanda. "The one Reeve found in the stunt car."

The conversation seemed to make Hatter dizzier than the trauma he had suffered. "Stunt car? What are you people talking about?" The unraveling of the murderer's note had transpired while Hatter was unconscious.

"Remember, at the end of our apprenticeship at Anderson's, how Damien had wanted to think up some final project for us—a chance to put our training to the test? Carter knew someone on the set of—"

"Yes, I remember. That movie they were filming. *Nine Man Morris*, right? Wait a minute! The note …"

The others confirmed the link between the note's "Nine Man's Murder" and the title of the film.

"That was the set that had the string of unexplained accidents involving the stuntman—"

"Julian Hayward."

"That's the one. The guy with the younger brother on the crew, the chubby makeup artist with long blond hair …"

"William Hayward," Bennett said.

"Wasn't he the one with that weird theory of Pinocchio?" Reeve asked. "That Pinocchio didn't become a real boy until Gepetto was swallowed by the whale?"

"A real oddball," Hatter said.

"William had a rough life," Jill pointed out in William's defense. "Always taken care of by his older brother, Julian. When they were children, Julian saved William from drowning in a stream. When William later torpedoed an artistic career by alienating his art teachers, Julian, a successful stunt man, got him hired in the industry as a makeup artist."

"What does all this have to do with Reeve and a ring?" Hatter asked.

Jonas summarized the sequence of events. Carter had a friend working on the crew of the film, *Nine Man Morris*, who had told him about a string of accidents involving Julian Hayward, whose stunt props were being sabotaged. Damien considered an investigation of the set a fitting final project for the graduating class.

Reeve's prime suspect had been another stuntman: Adam Burke, Julian Hayward's protégé. Hayward's mentoring had helped build Burke's reputation among producers and directors. There was even talk of replacing Hayward with the much younger Burke. Some thought Burke's debt to Hayward would inoculate Burke against disloyalty, but his ambition proved more potent than his gratitude. Reeve's theory of the accidents construed them as attempts by Burke to hasten his predecessor's retirement.

The trainees had been investigating for a week when someone tampered with the brakes of Julian Hayward's stunt car before a chase scene—fortunately, producing no injuries. Reeve's inspection of the sabotaged vehicle uncovered in the car's engine a gold ring, subsequently identified as Adam Burke's.

But just when the case seemed sewn up, a discovery of Bryan's opened a seam of doubt. Indulging a nagging suspicion, Bryan learned that one day before the accident (when the car's brakes had still been intact), Burke had, after removing his ring, injured the finger on which it had been worn. After Julian's car accident, Bryan tried unsuccessfully to place the ring on Burke's injured finger, which was too swollen to accept it.

If, Bryan argued, Burke had been wearing the ring when he had "sabotaged" the brakes, it could not possibly have fallen off the swollen finger. The ring, therefore, had been stolen and planted to incriminate Burke.

The one responsible for planting the ring, it turned out, was Reeve.

"You considered it more convenient to fabricate evidence than uncover it," Bryan reminded Reeve. "You never understood that you can't make the facts yield to you by bullying them into submission."

"When the facts don't fit," Reeve said, "you *make* them fit. As for Adam Burke, he was guilty. While you were all sitting around indulging your egos in fancy talk about inference and deduction, I was out catching a criminal."

"No one was ever convicted, if you recall," Amanda pointed out.

"My point exactly. Sometimes the only way to nab a culprit is to make creative use of your resources."

"Resources?" Bryan exclaimed. "Phony evidence is your idea of a resource? What about professional ethics?"

"Ethics? Look who's talking about ethics! Who was the one Damien took off the movie set case fifteen years ago, Bryan? Not me—*you*. And why? Breaking and entering.

"Let me tell you something about ethics, Mr. Holier-Than-Thou. I was just helping convict a criminal. But your interference cost me the career chance of a lifetime. I had been offered a job with Strathmore Investigations. I would have been a detective, not a babysitter for some underworld crime lord."

"Look," Gideon said, "that was a long time ago. I don't see what good it does to rake it all up again."

But Hatter had no intention of putting down the rake. "Perhaps," he told Reeve, "you didn't get the Strathmore job because you simply weren't smart enough for them."

Whatever had been capping Reeve's rage was blown off. "I'll *kill* you, Hatter—"

The grip of Bryan's and Jonas' hands around his wrists was all that stood between Reeve's wrath and Hatter's windpipe. It was not until Reeve's fury had subsided that Bryan and Jonas released him.

"Can we stop fighting among ourselves long enough to figure out what we're going to do?" Gideon asked. "There's a killer among us. How do we protect ourselves?"

"We stay together all weekend," Jonas said. "In the same room.

There's safety in numbers. What can one murderer do against seven people watching him?"

"You're crazy," Amanda said, "if you think I'm spending the night in a room with six men. I can take care of myself."

"Amanda's right," Reeve agreed. "I'm a bodyguard for the mob. I'm not afraid of some amateur."

"He's done all right so far."

"He got Damien when he was alone and not expecting anything. He got Carter before we started taking his note seriously. Now that we're on our guard, he's lost his key advantage."

Jill disagreed. "We all have to sleep sometime. I don't know about any of you, but I can't stay awake for three days straight. And I have no intention of falling asleep in a room with a murderer."

"We can take turns standing guard," Gideon suggested.

"And how do you know that the guard is not the killer?" Hatter asked. "You'll be letting the fox guard the henhouse."

"He's right," Bennett agreed. "Did you notice that among our provisions, all of the coffee and tea is decaf? There's no soda. No energy drinks. No chocolate. Nothing with caffeine. Nothing to help us stay awake. I may be speaking solely for myself, but if I fall asleep, I'd rather do so locked safely in my room than out here and vulnerable."

"Bennett may have a point," Bryan said. "If we lock the doors and windows of our rooms, what can the killer do? Bust down the door? I don't think so. Have you seen how these doors are constructed? Break a window? By the time the killer clears away the glass and climbs in, the victim will be out of the room. And the murderer will be identified and caught."

"*He* has the guns, remember?"

"Which he can use at any time. If we're all sitting ducks trying to capture him, imagine what that makes us just loitering here not even knowing who he is."

A vote decided the issue: The guests would barricade themselves in their rooms and stay alert. Yet no one left the parlor room.

31

Jill was feeling better. Still shaken, but much better than this morning. An almost unnatural calm had descended upon her, not unlike the comfort she knew as a child when Daddy, dashing and flirtatious, would ruffle her hair. *You take care of your family,* he had told her. *You protect the ones you love. Whatever it takes.*

Jill stared across the room at Bryan and felt the need for a drink. She gazed at the photograph of Imogen in the pendant Bryan had given her fifteen years ago. Imogen had sliced a path through the jungle of her dark soul. What could make up for Jill's loss, now that Imogen was gone?

As if sensing her pain, Amanda came over and joined her.

"You're thinking about Imogen, aren't you?" Amanda squeezed Jill's hand. "Don't worry, we'll get her back."

"I'm so sorry …"

"It wasn't your fault. Right now you're just overwrought. She's your daughter."

"She's *your* daughter, too."

"You've been raising her for five years. I know you think of her as your own."

"But you gave birth to her. And I'm—"

"We're going to get her back," Amanda assured her. "Whatever it takes."

It would be a slow death for each of them, Hatter thought. Slow enough for them to reflect on their lives, as on sleepless nights, regretting mistakes for which you can't forgive yourself. Like young Hatter choosing … no, wearing the same clothes and hairstyle as his peers, trying to be like everyone else, if only to please German parents who tried to fit into anti-German America between two world wars by becoming passionate conformists, changing their name from Kätte to the less German-sounding Cates. The crime of being no one.

Hatter had not been expecting Bennett to sit down a few feet from him on the sofa.

"I just want you to know that I *have* read some of your books," Bennett said.

"Oh?" Hatter replied cautiously. "And what did you think of them?"

"Fascinating. I was most impressed with the realistic detail," Bennett continued. "Especially the 'accidents' that keep befalling the characters who do not believe in the supernatural. It was like you were describing something you had seen with your own eyes."

Jonas, talking with Bryan and Gideon, glanced over at Hatter as the latter shifted his weight on the sofa.

"I also could not help but notice some fascinating coincidences," Bennett added.

"Coincidences?"

"In one of your books, *Spirits of the Dead*, a young woman spills salt, and shortly afterwards she slips off a subway platform into the path of an oncoming train. Eleven months before the book was published, the newspapers carried a story about a woman who fell off a platform in the L.A. Metro—police never determined if she fell or was pushed—and was killed on impact by the arriving train.

"In another one of your books, *Wednesday's Child*, an old man purposely steps on sidewalk cracks, when the steering and brakes of a passing truck mysteriously malfunction and the truck spins out of control, striking the man and killing him. A year before that book was released, a seventy-year-old man was walking home from the theater with his wife at 11:00 at night, when the emergency brake of a big rig parked on a hill suddenly went out. The truck rolled down the hill and hit the man, narrowly missing the wife. The old man died in the hospital seven hours later.

"There are countless other parallels between your novels and real-life accidents, involving black cats, broken mirrors, horseshoes, arson, boating accidents, and accidental shootings. But the most intriguing part is how closely the 'fictional' accidents in your novels resemble their real-life counterparts—not only the details of the accidents themselves, but the aftermaths as well. It's amazing how similarly everyone, fictional and real, is affected by the tragedies. It's almost as if you were there when the real-life accidents occurred and recorded everything in your books.

"But how could you possibly have been there? I mean, how would you know when and where accidents are going to occur? You would have to be psychic or something. How else can a person guarantee that he'll be at the scene of an accident when it happens?"

Bennett's brown eyes were strangely dull, though his evil grin told Hatter they should be twinkling. Hatter tried to meet those eyes with defiance.

Out of the corner of his eye Hatter caught sight of Jonas glancing in his direction.

WHAT WAS SO important, Reeve wondered, that Amanda needed to speak with him privately, in the dining room? Well, he was about to find out.

"I don't know how to say this tactfully," Amanda began, "so I'll just come right out and say it. You remember … the things we did together six years ago?"

"I have some vague recollection."

"Please, Reeve, don't make this harder for me than it already is. The thing is, there's something I never told you."

"You never told me why you simply disappeared."

"I'm telling you now. Reeve, I had a child. Your child."

"What?" Reeve finally managed to croak.

Amanda cast her eyes to the floor. "I'm sorry."

"Why didn't you tell me about it?"

"You don't understand. It's complicated."

"Give me the Cliff Notes."

"All right. I work for the D.A.'s office, Reeve—"

"You *what*?"

"I'm a deputy, but I've had my eye on assistant D.A. from the start. The thing is, my boss has some very strict views on promotion. He expects his assistant to have single-minded devotion to the job. He considers family a distraction. A woman with a husband—or, God forbid, a child—he would never even consider promoting.

"I've worked hard to get where I am, Reeve. I couldn't let a child get in the way. I couldn't let anyone know about it—not even you. I couldn't risk it."

"So what did you do? You didn't—"

"No. Of course not. The only person I told about it was Jill. I didn't know what else to do. And she made me an offer. She offered to raise my child—*our* child. For the last five years, Jill has been raising our daughter, Imogen."

Everything was happening too fast. Reeve's head felt like it had been swept up by a tornado.

"So why are you telling me about it now?"

For the first time, the cool, self-possessed deputy district attorney gave place to the panicky mother. "Oh, Reeve, they found out. They took her away—"

"Slow down."

"My hands are tied. If Peyton finds out what I did, my career is over. You're our only hope, Reeve. You're the child's father. You're the only way to hold onto her—"

Reeve bolted up from the dining table chair. "Now hold on a minute. Six years ago, you come to me out of the blue. You *give* yourself to me, for heaven's sake. Then you disappear, and now you tell me that you have a child, and I'm the father. What kind of game are you playing, Amanda? Why did you get involved with me to begin with? You never even liked me back at Anderson's. You were in love with …" Of course. "Is that it? Were you on the rebound from Jonas?"

"Don't be ridiculous. He had just become involved with …"

Too late Amanda clamped her lips.

"So that's it. He was in love with Jill fifteen years ago. Is that what happened? The man you loved got intimate with your best friend? And you licked your wounds by running to me?"

"What difference does it make, Reeve? All that matters now is that you're a father."

"I hate to break this to you, Amanda, but this is not a very good time for me to become a daddy. I'm kind of on the run from Antonio Capaldi. He thinks I betrayed him."

"Because of that key they found in the back room of the warehouse?"

"Someone had to have stolen that key from Capaldi's secret drawer. But the only people who even knew about the drawer were … Wait a minute. How did you know they found the key in the back room? I read all the accounts in the newspapers. None of them mentioned *where* in the warehouse the key was found."

"I work for the district attorney, remember? I have access to information like that."

"No, Amanda. I don't think so. I *told* you about that key … didn't I? I think *you* stole it and planted it in the warehouse. *That's* why you got involved with me. I was your bridge to Capaldi."

Amanda must have realized the futility of denial. "I'd been building a case against Capaldi, but when he destroyed the evidence in that warehouse, he destroyed all I had worked for. I had to improvise. I knew that key would lead us to Capaldi's coded ledger. It was an emergency backup plan.

"Thanks to a contact, I knew Capaldi intended to burn down the warehouse before we could get to it. But I had a warrant to search Capaldi's mansion. During the search, I was able to smuggle out the key. After Capaldi torched the warehouse, I went in and planted the key."

"I should have realized. Those questions you used to ask me … Oh, you were good. I never suspected the truth. Maybe I didn't want to."

"Reeve, I had an investigation to conduct. It was my job—"

"Your investigation forced Capaldi to set his own warehouse on fire. A man died in that fire, Amanda. The foreman—or at least we assume it was the foreman. His body was burned beyond recognition. And now your investigation has put my life in danger." Reeve headed for the doorway, turning his head as he passed through. "Good luck with your promotion."

32

It was all being raked up again, Gideon thought. The movie set. Their assignment. That night. The strange, clattering noise. The obscure set as he went off to investigate. And then all at once the ground below seeming to disappear … all support falling out from under him … the perilous drop …

He had turned to religion to find his footing. Religion would be his support, his sanctuary. He had memorized the Ten Commandments and the Beatitudes; the least sinful thought would set his fingers telling his rosary beads instinctively, without thinking.

Gideon had not even noticed Bennett seating himself in the chair a few feet from his wheelchair.

"You're not having second thoughts, are you?" Bennett asked.

"This is wrong. All of it. We should come clean."

"It's all going to be set straight," Bennett assured him.

"You lured me there under false pretenses. You said you needed my help."

"I did."

"You took advantage of me. I lost my calling because of you."

"I bailed you out of jail."

"You got me arrested to begin with." Gideon shifted his eyes away.

"We have a deal," Bennett said.

"And I expect you to keep up your end."

"Oh, I will. You'll know, I promise. Before the weekend is over."

There was a strange assurance in Bennett's voice. And then for the first time, it struck Gideon. Until now, he had been too preoccupied to notice.

"Everyone knows you're Bennett, not Aaron, now," Gideon said. "So why are you still—"

Jonas was approaching, eyeing them in a peculiar way.

A FATHER … RIGHT, Reeve thought, returning to his room. How could he be a father? He was a man on the run. Thank goodness he'd had the foresight to take out that "insurance policy." Happening to find out that Gideon was a priest had been a stroke of luck. But the rest was pure genius: Walking into the confessional that day and confessing his—and Capaldi's—illegal activities. Gideon now possessed secrets Capaldi would do anything to keep from the authorities. Of course, Gideon's knowledge would protect Reeve only as long as it was a threat Reeve held over Capaldi's head. Once that knowledge was revealed, Reeve would lose his leverage.

Fortunately, Gideon was bound by his oath to keep the words uttered in the confessional secret, no matter how strong his sense of duty to report them. Gideon would keep Reeve's secret for as long as Reeve was alive. But if something were to happen to Reeve, Gideon would be freed from his oath, wouldn't he? There would be nothing to stop him from reporting Capaldi's crimes to the police. And straight-laced Gideon would certainly report them. This was Capaldi's incentive to keep Reeve alive. As long as Capaldi knew that Reeve had confided in someone but didn't know who, he couldn't afford to harm Reeve.

Somehow Reeve had to find a way to let Capaldi know about this. Then he could finally stop running.

Something was wrong. He could tell the moment he entered his room. Something was there that had not been there before. He surveyed the room from the doorway. A sheet of paper was lying on the bed.

A note, folded in half.

> Reeve—
>
> Meet me in my room at midnight. Be discreet. Do not knock or say a word. Just enter quietly. Come alone. We have things to discuss.
>
> Mandy

Something had slipped out of the unfolded note and had fallen onto the bed. Reeve picked it up.

A key.

The key to Amanda's room?

Why would she want him to come to her room? To apologize for putting his life in danger? To make amends … ?

But she wanted something from him in return. He was the key to getting back that daughter of hers, she had said. Maybe she was using him all over again. Well, this time he wouldn't get taken in. This time, *he* would use *her*. One evening of pleasure—she owed him at least that much. And was apparently prepared to provide it.

Odd, though, that the note had been typewritten …

33

WONDERFUL TIMING, BRYAN. Bryan had arrived at his room as Jill was struggling with the lock of her bedroom door.

"Need any help?" Bryan asked.

"No. I'm fine."

Three days on a mountaintop with a murderer was preferable to three days of this. "What did I do now?"

Jill turned around. "Have you forgotten already? It was only two weeks ago."

"No, Jill, it started fifteen years ago. Sure, I was a playboy then, but I kicked the habit." Bryan lowered his eyes. "I can't help it that your father is Paul Templar."

"I know. My father set your mother up to take the fall. But he didn't kidnap Prissy, and he didn't injure her or kill your parents."

"Look, Jill. I don't want to blame him."

"I know, Bryan. You *need* to blame him."

AMANDA WAS FEELING sleepy as she mounted the dimly lit staircase. It had taken forever to break free of Bennett trying to be friendly.

Poor Reeve. Amanda could imagine how he must feel. But she couldn't have told him about Imogen five years ago—she just couldn't. And she couldn't have just abandoned Imogen to some orphanage. Thank God Jill had insisted on helping. Amanda could never have risked doing to Imogen what her parents had done to her.

Though it was Mom that Dad abused, primarily, Amanda had still been a victim of that abuse. Until Mom finally fled with Amanda; but by then Mom's emotional scars were too deep. When Amanda was taken away, she bounced from foster home to foster home until finally being adopted at age twelve. How could Amanda ever hope to be a good parent, when her own parents had not been?

What was happening? The lights were suddenly smothered, covering the staircase with a suffocating dark.

If she could only silence the swish of her flouncy white dress as she climbed the stairs. For here in this black stillness, the barely discernible sound seemed to echo toward the waiting ears of someone concealed in the dark.

Where was he hiding? Amanda felt her body stiffen as she sensed the presence of someone behind her. She opened her mouth to cry out. But it was too late.

Powerful fingers wrapped around her throat like snakes, tightening their coils with cold-blooded reflex. She tried to scream, but a hand sealed her mouth.

Her struggle dislodged the madman's grasp long enough to permit a distress call to escape. It was answered by a chorus of voices from above and below.

"Did you hear that?"

"Sounded like it came from the stairs."

Heavy footfalls on the staircase drummed into her brain a welcome realization. Her assailant had released his grip and fled.

"Someone get the lights."

Her hand rose to soothe her chafing neck, but any hoped-for relief was struck down by a body colliding with hers. The light snapped on. Jonas was standing above her, looking down. Reeve was running across the upstairs hall toward her. A bedroom door opened; Hatter stuck out his head, peering into the hallway cautiously. Bennett was mounting the staircase, followed by Bryan and Jill.

"Mandy, what happened?" Jill asked.

"Someone attacked me. Tried to strangle me." Amanda sat on the stair, trying to control her trembling.

"Let's have a look at you." Jonas knelt beside her.

"I'm all right," Amanda insisted. She would not let him near.

"What's going on up there?" Gideon called from the base of the stairway.

"Someone tried to kill Amanda. She's all right."

"Well, it's getting lonely down here." Gideon's voice sounded shaky. "Why don't you come downstairs, since I can't come up to you?"

Slowly they descended the staircase.

34

AMANDA SAT ALONE on the drawing room sofa, refusing to lie down. Rest would relax her less than an unobstructed view of the others.

"Well, at least things are beginning to look up," declared the ever-optimistic Gideon. "It's the second time the killer has slipped up. That's two failed attempts in a row."

Bryan eyed him coolly. "I wouldn't write him off quite yet."

"I agree with Gideon," Reeve said. "The killer has obviously set himself a task he's not equal to."

Bryan turned to Amanda. "How are you holding up, Manly?" he asked. "Jill, would you get Amanda a bottle of water? Sealed, of course."

Jill left for the kitchen.

Amanda was looking at Bryan. "You haven't called me 'Manly' since—"

"You insisted on inspecting the scaffolding."

Fifteen years ago, the crew of *Nine Man Morris* had created a building construction site for a scene involving several stunts. Amanda and Jonas had volunteered to inspect the scaffolding for signs of tampering, but Damien had been reluctant to let a "girl" risk her safety.

"But you insisted that anything a man could do, a woman could do as well," Jonas remembered.

"That's when you started calling me 'Manly,'" Amanda said to Bryan.

Bennett glanced around. "Wasn't that scaffolding the scene of …"

"The accident. Yes."

That day Julian Hayward, the senior stuntman, had been performing stunts on the scaffolding. But something went wrong. One of the beams gave way under him, sending him plummeting to his death.

"It was not even supposed to have been Julian's scene," Bennett recalled. "Adam Burke had been the stuntman for that sequence."

"That's right," Reeve said. "Burke had injured his leg that morning and couldn't perform the stunt."

Julian Hayward's protégé and rival, Adam Burke, had been carousing until late the night before. Stepping out of the elevated door of the trailer he had slept in until early afternoon, Burke sustained a fall that left him with a twisted ankle—an hour before he was to have performed a stunt.

"The director was just shooting cover shots that afternoon, mainly," Bennett recalled quietly, "so he substituted Julian for Burke."

"I'll never forget that day," Amanda said. That morning she had been alone with the director in his office when William Hayward, Julian's makeup artist brother, entered. The actors had been complaining that the makeup was taking too long to apply.

"If you would provide the proper supplies," William told the director, "it wouldn't take so long."

The argument was interrupted by a phone call. The three-member construction crew was supposed to complete work on the scaffolding that morning. One of them had called in sick and would not be coming in. No replacement could be found on such short notice. The director was vexed by the thought of further delay in a film already behind schedule.

"A delay might have saved Julian Hayward's life," Jonas remarked.

"William took Julian's death really hard," Bennett recalled. "Shortly after the accident, William suffered a complete nervous breakdown and was committed to Lakeview. An acquaintance of mine who works there told me that for long periods at a stretch, William refused to eat anything, till it completely altered his appearance. "

Gideon nodded. "Even before the accident, William told me, he had been having nightmares in which terrible things would happen to Julian."

Jill reentered the drawing room, water bottle in hand.

Amanda stood abruptly. "I don't need anything to drink. I just need to get some rest. If I can."

"If you can't sleep, try counting blessings," Gideon said.

Jill looked up. "Where have I heard that before?"

"It's a proverb they used to use in my parish when I was a priest." Too late Gideon realized his blunder.

"What?" Reeve barked.

"What are you talking about, Gideon?" Jill asked.

"I … they took away my collar."

"Why?"

Gideon glanced helplessly at Bennett. "I got into some … trouble. I really can't talk about it."

Reeve glared at Gideon. "Are you saying that you're no longer a priest?"

"Look, Reeve, I—"

"And when did you plan to tell me about this?"

"It's a misunderstanding. It will be cleared up."

"And what about those things I told you? Are they no longer protected by your oath of secrecy?"

Amanda began to comprehend. "Reeve, you didn't—"

"What's going on here?" Jill asked.

Amanda kept her eyes fixed on Reeve. "I'm guessing, Reeve, that you fed Gideon incriminating information about Capaldi under the protection of the confessional, thinking that the threat of exposure will keep Capaldi off your back—"

"Reeve's on the run from Capaldi?"

"— without the risk of Gideon revealing the information prematurely."

"But now that Gideon is no longer a priest—" Hatter began.

Reeve skewered Gideon with his eyes. "Well, what happens now?"

"I don't know, Reeve. They don't exactly teach you what to do when you're defrocked. Somehow it's not covered in seminary."

Hatter chuckled cruelly. "A brilliant plan, up in smoke."

The words seemed to trigger a chain reaction in Jonas' mind. "Unless ..." All eyes fastened upon him. "Unless Reeve has a backup plan. You may have unwittingly hit the nail on the head just now, Hatter. Capaldi set his warehouse on fire. A man was killed in that fire. It was assumed that he was the warehouse foreman, though his body was burned beyond recognition. If Capaldi is after Reeve, Reeve knows he'll never relent as long as Reeve is alive. But if he thinks Reeve is dead—"

"Of course!" Bryan finished for Jonas. "Reeve stages a 'reunion' and murders all the guests. He then burns the bodies beyond recognition—including that of Damien, who, like Reeve, is a large man. Capaldi will assume Reeve was one of the victims and break off the chase."

"Then why warn his victims?" Jill asked.

"Battle of wits."

"You're crazy, Bryan," Reeve said.

"Well, I don't know about any of you," Hatter declared, "but I don't plan to let Reeve—or anyone else—win that battle."

35

AMANDA WAS TOO far away to tell for sure. The moment she flipped on her room light, her hand shot to her mouth. Was it nerves, or was something there? Slowly, cautiously, she approached.

It was real, all right. Something was lying on the writing table. Something small, silver, shiny.

A handgun.

All of the guns had disappeared that afternoon; now one of them had rematerialized in her room. Who had put it here? And why?

She examined it. Three bullets inside.

WHAT WAS HE going to do about Gideon? Reeve wondered. Killing them all and burning their bodies beyond recognition—was that really the only way? Not that they deserved any better. After all, it was their fault he was in this predicament to begin with. If it weren't for them, he wouldn't have been working for Capaldi in the first place. When they exposed his planting of that ring in the stunt car, Reeve's career as a detective was cut short. No one would hire him. It made him want to strike out at the world—one, two, one, two. But it was his ethics being questioned, not his brains. He knew all about logic: finding tangible proof for your theories. When a crime won't yield to your theories, you resort to logic.

But look where it had gotten him. Blackballed as a detective. Fortunately, it was Antonio Capaldi who had been backing production of *Nine Man Morris*—one of his many money laundering fronts—and when Capaldi saw how Reeve was not afraid to take the initiative, he hired Reeve as a bodyguard, not long after graduation.

Of course, look how that turned out.

Almost midnight. Amanda had given him no sign, no acknowledgment of their impending meeting. Well, she was probably still shaken by the attack. An anxious thought: Would that prevent the rendezvous from taking place? No. He could bring her around.

She had not let Jonas look her over. Odd. Reeve had paid little heed at the time, had made no attempt to discern any marks on her neck. He regretted that now. Was it possible that she was setting him up? That there *were* no marks on her neck … because no one had attacked her? Because *she* was the murderer, luring the next victim to her lair?

After all, she was not behaving like a woman on the threshold of a tryst. And then the note itself: *"Do not knock. Don't say a word."* Exactly what it would say, if it were a prelude to murder.

No, she wouldn't try to kill him. She needed him, to get back that daughter of hers. Or was that what she wanted him to believe, to disarm him, to take him off his guard? This killer had shown himself to be shrewd, and Amanda, Reeve knew, fit that bill. Perhaps he should ask Jill about it, to see if she'd verify the story.

Tomorrow he'd ask. For tonight, he would play along. But until he knew one way or the other, he would exercise every caution.

Now that was odd: He hadn't noticed *that* before. The fireplace poker from the drawing room. Someone had propped it against the wall beside his bedroom door. Had it been there earlier? Reeve couldn't remember.

Still, he told himself, *don't let an overactive imagination ruin what could be a promising evening.*

However, a little precaution would do no harm.

He pocketed the key to Amanda's room, wrapped his fingers around the poker, and poked his head cautiously, noiselessly, into the upstairs hallway.

How long had she been standing there, staring at the gun? Time had seemed to stop, until she heard an unexpected scratching. It sounded like … a key entering a lock. Amanda fixed her eyes on the door. A click. Someone had unlocked her door. The knob turned. As the creaking door began to creep across the floor, a silhouette inched its way into the room.

Her fears scattered in panic like wild geese startled by a gunshot. What should she do? *The lights. Flip off the room light. Switch on the desk lamp. Aim it at the door.* Darkness hid her from stalking eyes, but would offer no such harbor to her stalker, who would walk right into the spotlight—and the sights of her pointed gun.

A dark shadow pierced the edge of the light: a hand, armed with some kind of … rod, or other weapon. Scouting out possible danger to its owner, who had come to finish the job he had begun earlier, on the staircase.

Well, not this time.

She waited for his chest to round the door's edge. Then she pulled the trigger.

36

The inn was flooded with light and footsteps flowing toward Amanda's room, where a circle of leaden eyes stared down at the prone body of a man. Jonas knelt and flipped it over: Reeve.

"Shot to death."

"I found the gun here," Amanda muttered. "Then the door creaked open. He crept in, with that … fire poker. I thought … I thought he had come to …"

Jonas turned his attention back to the corpse. From a pocket of Reeve's sporty shirt he produced a slip of paper. The invitation to Amanda's room.

"What happened now?" Gideon's voice called up the stairs.

"Fill him in, will you?" Jonas asked Jill, who drifted to the head of the staircase.

"Reeve is dead," Jill called out. "Amanda shot him ... in self-defense."

"Make sure he's dead," Gideon suggested.

"Jonas already did."

"Check again. I once read a murder mystery in which a group of people are murdered one by one. It turns out that one of them is actually only pretending to be dead—and he's the murderer."

Jill returned to Amanda's room. "He said—"

"I heard what he said." Jonas indicated the body. "Be my guest."

"Thanks, I'd rather not."

"Hatter?"

Hatter's examination confirmed Jonas' diagnosis. So did Bryan's and Bennett's.

"I know what you're all thinking," Jonas said. "Carter. I wasn't the only one to examine him. You did too, Bryan."

"He was dead, all right," Bryan concurred.

Amanda, who had also examined Carter's dead body, stood apart, nodding like a marionette.

"What about Damien?" Bennett asked.

Bryan's eyes dipped imperceptibly in fleeting homage. "You are referring, no doubt, to the fact that the knife wound through his abdomen had scarcely bled. I didn't *think* I was the only one to have noticed that. But I examined him carefully, and he was dead."

"I examined him, too," Jonas said. "Definitely dead."

"Absolutely," agreed Hatter.

"I also noticed a wound on Damien's head," Bryan added, "which appeared to have been made by a blunt object."

Meanwhile Jonas checked Reeve's pockets, producing two keys. He tried both keys in Amanda's door. Only one locked and unlocked it.

"The other is the key to Reeve's room, I assume." Jonas turned to Amanda. "Where's your key, Amanda?"

"I thought I had misplaced it. For a while, with all the excitement, it slipped my mind. After the murders, I didn't think it wise to advertise the fact."

Jonas handed Amanda the key with which he had locked and

unlocked her door. "It appears you didn't lose it. The murderer stole it from you and gave it to Reeve. That's how Reeve got through your door, assuming you locked it."

"But how did the—?"

Amanda did not complete the question. Instead, she tested the key in her door lock, confirming it was indeed her room key.

The men turned their attention to Reeve's body.

"I guess this means burying another one," Hatter said.

37

BRYAN TOSSED ANOTHER log onto the fire, to beat back the morning chill. He briefly considered adding to the fire the balsa wood detonator box sitting on the mantle. The box was bone dry, as it had been when Carter had found it yesterday, and would burn nicely. But no, it was evidence of a sort. Fixed on the box, Bryan's eyes saw nothing else; and it was only a noise from behind that freed him from the grip of thought. Jill had tried to enter the drawing room quietly, apparently craving the warmth of the fire more than wishing to avoid a confrontation with Bryan.

She was dressed simply in snug-fitting red corduroy slacks and white pullover sweater, blonde hair seeming to charm light from the fire. On Jill, even the most casual clothing looked elegant.

Bryan had dallied not so much with women as with their acceptance; after Jill, he gave them up cold turkey. He didn't blame Jill for the breakup. He couldn't expect her to stay with him while he went after her father. But he couldn't just abandon his quest to avenge his family, either.

Yet after seven years of building an investigative empire, his goal of driving Paul Templar out of business began to cool in the chilling prospect of life without Jill. So Bryan tracked her down, prepared to give up the crusade. Her door was answered by an old woman who told Bryan Jill was at work.

"You must be Jill's young man," the old woman said.

Jill's young man. So Jill had found someone else. And Bryan cared enough about her not to complicate her life.

He stayed away for three years. That was all he could manage. Perhaps the relationship with the "young man" had fizzled out. Bryan would keep his visit secret, however, until he knew for sure.

What he saw through the bedroom window squashed his hopes. A baby's crib. Apparently Jill had settled down and was raising a family. There was no place in her life for Bryan.

But that did not keep him way. For five years he would "visit," at a distance, watching Jill's beautiful daughter grow up before his eyes. That was how he had recognized the girl two weeks ago.

Jill stood by the drawing room fire in silence.

"I'm going to help you get your daughter back," Bryan promised.

"Just let it go, Bryan. Haven't you done enough already?"

"I was trying to help. I didn't know it would create a problem. I still don't know why they took her away. Some kind of welfare fraud, is all I was able to learn. Whatever is going on, you have the authorities completely baffled." Bryan's tone sobered. "Look, Jill, I saw your daughter—"

"Her name's Imogen."

"I was at the downtown police station looking into a case, when suddenly officers brought in this five-year-old girl they had found wandering in front of the psychic fair next door, crying for her mommy. In her pocket they had discovered a key that had just been stolen from the evidence locker of that very police station. The girl was terrified. I recognized her. I thought by identifying her—"

"How did you know who she was? You've been spying on me, haven't you? If you had just stayed away like I'd asked fifteen years ago ... but no, you weren't content to ruin my father. You had to take my daughter from me, too."

Anger swept Jill from the drawing room along a collision course with Jonas in the entry hall.

"Whoa, what's wrong, Jill?"

"Nothing, Jonas, just let me pass."

"Bryan? Still? After all he's done to you? I tried to warn you fifteen years ago."

"Bryan wanted me. Whatever else you can say about him, he wanted me. With you I always felt like the Golden Glass Award."

"An award *he* coincidentally won."

"You're every bit as good a detective as Bryan, and you know it."

"Bryan has awards to show for it."

"You're not Bryan."

Jonas stepped back, as if struck.

"I never meant to hurt you, Jonas," Jill said. "I just couldn't feel the way you did."

"What about what happened between us eight years ago?"

"That was ... I was confused."

"Sounds like you still are."

Jonas left Jill in the hallway and entered the drawing room.

"I see you haven't lost your inimitable charm," he said to Bryan.

"I take it you ran into Jill."

"Literally."

Bryan fidgeted, stabbing the fire with the fire poker, the one they had found beside Reeve's body the night before. "I think I can guess the topic of conversation."

"Actually, we were talking about the Golden Glass Award." The Golden Glass was a gold-plated trophy—shaped like a magnifying glass—awarded annually to the private investigator credited with the year's best achievement. "And the fact that it was *you* who won it."

"You didn't want it, Jonas. You didn't lift a finger to get it. You never even *talked* about it until there was speculation that I might receive it."

You're always looking behind, Bryan used to tell him. *Not moving toward something, but away from something.*

"So what are we going to do now?" Jonas asked, wrenching his thoughts back to the present. "Any ideas?"

"Right now, more questions than answers. From the very beginning certain aspects of this affair have troubled me."

"Like the fact that two men drove us here, rather than one?"

"As a matter of fact," Bryan confessed, "that's one of them. What are your thoughts?"

"We don't seem to be suffering from an overabundance of clues. I'd like to get my hands on that cigarette lighter that mysteriously disappeared from Bennett's pocket."

As if conjured by the mention of his name, Bennett appeared in the doorway. He still wore the stained white overalls upon which Jill had spilled wine the day before. He entered the drawing room but kept a distance from the two men.

"I just passed Jill going into her room," Bennett said. "She seemed more upset than usual."

"Just a spat with Bryan," Jonas said.

"Well, Bryan, she's still a pretty girl." Bennett grinned. "If you need a stand-in, I'd be glad to volunteer."

Bryan watched him coldly. "You would probably not be my first choice, Bennett," Bryan said, "since you are the cause of my current problem."

Bennett raised an eyebrow. "What are you talking about?"

"I'm talking about the theft of Antonio Capaldi's ledger from the evidence locker of the downtown L.A. police station two weeks ago. There were two thieves. One—the one police believe to be the mastermind—got away. They captured his accomplice. A man in a wheelchair. I'm guessing that was Gideon. The way he's been acting. The fact that he's suddenly been defrocked. Priests don't often get defrocked. But getting caught committing a felony—possibly a federal offense—will do that."

Bennett kept eyes locked on Bryan. "What does that have to do with me?"

"I think you're the mastermind. Those conspiratorial whispers you and Gideon have been exchanging. I'm right, aren't I?"

"The cat's out of the bag," Gideon said as he wheeled himself into the drawing room. "We may as well come clean."

But Bennett betrayed no interest in baring his soul. "Bennett tricked me," Gideon said. "He told me he needed my help—he didn't say with what. I accompanied him to the police station. It turns out that Bennett is a freelance smuggler. Antonio Capaldi hired him to steal some evidence from the downtown police station.

"Bennett had a contact at the station, who left him a copy of the key to the evidence locker. Once inside the locker, Bennett stole a book—some kind of ledger—and hid it under the cushion of my wheelchair. He needed me to be the vehicle for smuggling out the book. I must have looked nervous, because they stopped me and searched the wheelchair. They found the ledger. Bennett fled."

"The convention center hosting the psychic fair was right next door to the police station," Bryan told Bennett. "You fled into the crowd in front of the fair. You knew you might be caught, and you didn't want the incriminating locker key found on you. So you ducked it into the pocket of a five-year-old girl wandering in the crowd. That girl was Imogen, Jill's daughter."

"What does all this have to do with you?" Bennett asked.

"Everything," Bryan said.

38

In the parlor room, after breakfast, Amanda was cross-examined about her shooting of Reeve the night before.

"Did you write that note to Reeve?" Gideon asked.

"Don't be absurd," Amanda said.

"I've been thinking about that note." Jonas addressed the group. "The person who wrote it must have left it somewhere for Reeve to find—"

"So Reeve came into Amanda's room for what he thought would be—" Gideon flushed slightly. "— a rendezvous?"

"But how do you explain the fire poker?" Jill asked. "The one we found next to Reeve's body?"

"Perhaps Reeve was suspicious," Bennett suggested, "and brought it along for protection, just in case."

"He *should* have been suspicious," Bryan said dryly. "Amanda's 'invitation' had been typed. But there's no typewriter at Moon's End, only that computer printer in the study. And if Reeve had bothered trying to print something with it—as I did this morning—he'd have discovered that its cartridge is out of ink. Amanda couldn't have typed that note here at Moon's End. Which means she would have had to come here with the note already printed. Can you see Amanda doing that?"

Hatter directed at Amanda his most barbed tone. "How do we know you didn't plant that fire poker next to Reeve's body yourself? To make it look like you killed him in self-defense?"

"You're missing the big picture, Hatter," Jonas interjected. "See how it all fits together. The person who planted that note for Reeve also put the gun in Amanda's room—"

"Or so she claims."

"That same person attacked Amanda earlier last night. He didn't 'botch' the attempt, as Reeve had thought. He never intended to kill her."

"He just wanted to shake you up," Bryan told Amanda, "so that when Reeve entered your room at midnight—drawn there by the note the killer had left—you would be jumpy. And would use the gun the killer had planted there. Our murderer probably also provided the fire poker for Reeve to arm himself with—further ensuring that you would consider Reeve a hostile intruder."

"You were manipulated, Mandy," Jonas concluded, "and you behaved precisely as the killer had anticipated. He got you to kill one of his victims for him."

"At least the deaths have all been instantaneous," Bennett pointed out. "Reeve being shot, Carter poisoned, and Damien stabbed." He shrugged. "They all died quickly, if that's worth anything."

"Maybe the note to Reeve can tell us more," Gideon suggested. "Something we may have overlooked. May I have another look at it?"

Everyone denied having it.

"I gave it to Bennett last night," Jill said.

"And I gave it to Hatter."

"I put it on the cabinet in the dining room last night," Hatter replied, "when I went for something to eat."

Gideon started to maneuver his wheelchair.

"I'll get it," Jill said, passing through the doorway before Gideon had even turned to face it.

"Well, at least our list of suspects is dwindling," Gideon said dryly. "Two are dead; and we know the murderer is someone who attacked Amanda and tried to poison Hatter. So we're narrowing it down."

"Aren't you making a dubious assumption?" Hatter asked.

"Such as?"

"That the killer is one of us?"

"We searched the entire mountaintop," Bennett insisted. "There's no one up here but us."

"No one alive ..."

An explanation, if Hatter had intended to provide one, was forestalled by Jill's return with a folded slip of paper.

"It was on the cabinet, where you left it," she told Hatter, handing the note to Gideon.

"What did you mean by that remark ...?" Bennett asked Hatter in a shaky voice. "No one alive?"

"Isn't it obvious? This is not the work of any human being."

"Oh my God," Gideon gasped. He gaped at the note dangling from his hand. "It's not the same note."

39

"May I?" Jonas took the note from Gideon and read it aloud.

> "WHO WILL BE NEXT? WHOSE NAME NOW HEADS THE LIST? WATCH YOUR STEP . . . FOR THE NEXT VICTIM HAS ALREADY BEEN CHOSEN. IN FACT, I HAVE A SPECIAL SURPRISE IN STORE FOR HIM: ONE HE'LL NEVER GUESS, THOUGH I'M SURE HE'LL TAKE A STAB AT IT.
>
> "AND THEN THE REST OF YOU.

"FIRST I'LL DESTROY YOUR LIVES . . . THEN YOUR REPUTATIONS. I'LL CHRONICLE YOUR PATHETIC, FRUITLESS STRUGGLE AGAINST ME—PERHAPS EVEN PUBLISH IT IN A BOOK AND EXPOSE YOUR INCOMPETENCE FOR ALL THE WORLD TO SEE, BLACKENING YOUR NAMES FOREVER. AND NO ONE WILL BE AROUND TO SUE ME FOR SLANDER.

"TIME IS RUNNING OUT. ONLY HOURS LEFT TO UNMASK THE KILLER . . . AND THEN, THE DEADLY CLIMAX. BECAUSE BEFORE THE WEEKEND FADES TO BLACK, EVERY PERSON AT MOON'S END—EXCEPT ONE—WILL BE DEAD."

The typewritten message was passed around for all to analyze.

"And let's get this right on the first take this time," Bennett suggested, "before there are more deaths."

Bryan fixed his eyes on Bennett. "This killer is obviously someone who enjoys toying with his victims," he observed, "like a cat toys with its prey."

"And your point is?" Bennett asked.

"If we look around for someone deriving similar enjoyment at our expense, what do we find? You seemed to enjoy that little game with Aaron, the mute caretaker, and the mysterious noise outside."

"Because I did," Bennett replied. "What do you want me to do, pretend I care what happens to any of you? After what you all did to me?"

Everyone understood the reference. While working the movie set case, Bennett had been smitten with an actress named Dolores, who did not return his affection. So it was easy for Bennett's fellow trainees to put her up to a practical joke. She allowed Bennett to "figure out" her guilt in the sabotaged stunts, then "confessed" to him in private.

"You won't turn me in, will you, Bennett?" she'd pleaded.

Bennett had promised not to, before discovering the humiliating prank.

"Revenge is a powerful motive for murder," Bryan pointed out.

"I came here to make fools of you," Bennett said. "Not kill you. Besides, one of you is after *me*."

"What are you talking about?"

"A week ago an anonymous note appeared in my mailbox. It said, '*Who can piece together your little mishap at the police station? Who knows about your connection to Antonio Capaldi, because they had a connection to him fifteen years ago and have, in one way or another, never escaped his influence? Who knew you as Bennett Nash—before all of your smuggler's aliases—and can finger you to the police, as well as to Capaldi?*'"

"Bennett, you're being paranoid," Amanda said. "Someone is putting these ideas in your head to manipulate you."

"And you always go along without question," Hatter added.

They dredged up an example of Bennett's suggestibility. Toward the end of their investigation on the set of *Nine Man Morris*, the detectives had been searching for a peg removed from a breakaway railing, causing Julian Hayward to fall prematurely while shooting a stunt—fortunately without injuries onto a safety mat below. Reeve had suspected Adam Burke of trying to create the appearance that Hayward had lost his balance—part, Reeve felt, of a plan to erode Hollywood's confidence in the veteran and hasten Hayward's replacement by Burke.

Reeve shared this theory with Bennett, who decided the missing peg would not be found far from Adam Burke—so enthusiastically that, at five o'clock in the morning, he conducted an extensive (many thought, obsessive) search for the peg, culminating underneath Adam Burke's trailer. Though large wooden planks surrounding the base of the trailer barred access, a movable set of wooden stairs below the door concealed a crawlspace beneath the trailer. Bennett's search under the trailer, however, produced nothing but ridicule.

"If I recall," Jill said, "that was the same morning as …"

"As Julian's fatal fall," Jonas finished for her. Jill had not been in the room when they had discussed it the day before.

"I still remember that day," Jill said. "I didn't actually see him fall, but I remember watching the construction workers come onto the set earlier that morning to finish work on the scaffolding. Their somber gray overalls and hard hats. Funny, the details that stick in your mind. And I recall watching them work and thinking, If that scaffolding is safe enough for those three construction workers, it's certainly safe enough for one stunt man." Jill shivered. "Only a few hours later Julian Hayward fell from it to his death."

Amanda watched Jill as closely as Bennett was watching Amanda.

"That's very interesting," Amanda said slowly. "You never mentioned that before …" After a moment, she added, "I think I'd like to be alone for a while … and rest …"

"Mandy, stay with us," Jill called as Amanda left the room.

"Let her go," Jonas said.

A mental fog spread to engulf everyone, for their talk led them in circles, rehashing last night's attack on Amanda and the murder of Reeve. The circle was finally broken by the ghostly reappearance of Amanda in the parlor room doorway.

"The gun I used last night," she muttered. "It's gone."

"WE ALWAYS SEEM to be one step behind," Gideon observed.

"Haven't any of you realized yet *why* the killer is always one step ahead?" Hatter asked. "Why objects keep disappearing before our eyes? Don't you see why we can't catch him? Because we can't see him. We can't see *it*. It has to be a ghost."

"A ghost," Jonas repeated dryly.

"The spirits of those who meet with violent ends find no rest until they have been avenged."

"And which ghost is seeking vengeance up here?" Bryan asked.

"That's a good question. Which of us has been associated with a wrongful death?" Hatter studied Bryan. "We all know how your parents died, Bryan; and Jill was connected with those deaths, since it was her father who helped bring them about."

"This is ridiculous, Hatter—"

"Is it, Amanda? What about Reeve? He worked for Antonio Capaldi, who torched his own warehouse, killing the foreman. An event you were associated with, too, Amanda."

"Well, *I'm* not associated with a wrongful death," Jonas pointed out.

"Carter was," Jill whispered.

"Yes, his brother was murdered up here." Hatter turned to Bennett. "And this morning I heard you and Gideon confess your roles in the theft of Capaldi's ledger from the police evidence locker."

"But no one died," Gideon protested.

"Actually," Jonas corrected, "when the police chased Bennett into the crowd, they thought he was drawing a weapon on them. One of them fired at him and killed an innocent bystander."

"You were involved in that death, too, Hatter," Amanda pointed out. "The crowd had gathered outside the psychic fair, where you were one of the speakers."

"This is silly," Gideon said. "Forgive me, Hatter, but I can't help but feel we should be able to come up with a more rational explanation for what's happening up here. After all, we were trained as private detectives. Damien gave each of us a thorough knowledge of criminal investigation."

Bryan added, with unusual emphasis, "As well as a detailed background in all major aspects of criminal and civil law. With our training, we ought to be able to figure this out, without having to resort to supernatural explanations."

"Like we solved our graduation assignment?" Hatter taunted. "Remember how that ended."

"With Julian's death," Jill muttered.

"Which *you* didn't see," Hatter pointed out. "How is that, Jill? The *rest* of us saw the accident. Where were *you* when Julian Hayward fell?"

"I was questioning his brother, William, in the makeup department. It was so easy to get sidetracked watching William work. He could make an actor look like anyone. One time, when an actor didn't show up, William himself stood in for him. He fooled everyone on the set with his disguise—until he started talking. He could do great faces, but not voices—"

"Where is all of this getting us?" Bennett blurted out impatiently.

"It's just that I could never really question William," Jill replied. "So, on the morning of Julian's death—before it happened, actually—I cornered William while he was working. At that time neither of us knew about Burke's twisted ankle, his replacement by Julian, or Julian's fall. After the accident, William broke down."

"William Hayward was never particularly stable to begin with," Hatter said. "Even before Julian's death, he was seeing a psychiatrist, who told him there are no accidents, because unconscious motivations underlie everything we do."

"There's a pattern here, you know," Bryan said. "Don't you find it interesting that the sabotaged stunts involving Julian Hayward—like the disabled stunt car and railing—were all harmless? None of them were ever *really* dangerous. While the one sabotaged stunt that was to have involved Adam Burke turned out to be fatal."

"Aren't you forgetting that it *wasn't* Adam Burke who was killed in that stunt?" Jonas pointed out.

"I see what you're getting at," Gideon said. "Maybe it was only meant to *look* like the sabotage had been intended for Burke."

"You mean Burke knew the stunt had been rigged," Hatter asked, "because *he* had rigged it? And faked the injury to his leg, so that Hayward would be the one to perform it?"

"And so, by making it look like *he* was the intended victim," Gideon concluded, "Burke would go unsuspected, apparently blameless."

"Except for one thing," Amanda pointed out. "Killing is a crime."

"Murder is a sin," Bennett amended darkly.

Jonas sewed together their argument. "So Burke sabotages his own stunt, then fakes an injury to his leg. Julian Hayward—the *real* victim—is substituted for Burke. Burke's rival is thus eliminated, and Burke is made to look like the intended victim, rather than the perpetrator." Jonas looked at Bryan. "Reeve was right all along."

Bryan looked as convinced as an atheist at a revival meeting. "Except for one thing. That's not the way it happened."

Jonas' objection was more academic than antagonistic. "And how do you know that?"

"Because I just now realized the truth. Let's put together what we know. First, Adam Burke had been out drinking late the night before. The next day he slept in until early afternoon, stepped out of the door of his trailer—which was three feet above the ground—fell, and twisted his ankle.

"Now, we also know that earlier that same morning Bennett had been snooping around Adam Burke's trailer, searching for a peg missing from a sabotaged railing, which had broken under Julian's weight a day or two before. Bennett even searched *under* the trailer—a fact we haven't exactly allowed him to live down.

"Now think about how those trailers were constructed. The bottoms were barricaded by large wooden planks. The only way for Bennett to have gotten under the trailer was to have moved aside the wooden steps below the entrance and entered through the crawlspace behind them."

Bryan turned to Bennett. "You moved those steps away from the door—*but you forgot to move them back*. When Burke emerged from his trailer that afternoon—dazed from a hangover—there were no steps there. That's why he fell three feet and twisted his ankle. It was because of you that Hayward was substituted for Burke during that fatal stunt. In a way, *you* were responsible for Julian Hayward's death."

"Oh no," Bennett fumed. "You can't blame this on me. I won't be your scape … I had nothing to do with it." Eyeing each guest in turn, he added cryptically, "But I *know* who killed Julian."

Fury swept him from the room like a feather in a hurricane.

"Perhaps we should give tempers a chance to cool," Bryan suggested. "Separately."

Jill disagreed. "I think we should stick together, especially now."

"Look what happens when we're together," Jonas pointed out. "Tempers flare. It happened yesterday with Reeve, remember? And now he's dead."

"Maybe that's what the murderer is counting on," Gideon agreed.

"Turning us against one another. Perhaps to use us, like he used Amanda to kill Reeve last night."

"But splitting up will make us more vulnerable," Hatter protested.

"We split up last night," Amanda said. "And we all survived."

"Except Reeve."

"He left his room."

"But what about safety in numbers?"

"We were all together at dinner last night when Carter was killed," Jonas argued. "Being together doesn't make us safe."

It was decided that a short break might clear everyone's head. It was daytime, and the murderer seemed to prefer striking at night.

And so the group disintegrated, scattering like dust in a storm.

41

To her surprise, Jill actually felt relieved to be alone, with no one to keep an eye on—and no one keeping an eye on her—as she emerged from the kitchen, a sealed water bottle in hand. She entered the empty parlor room, en route to her bedroom.

The sound of footsteps in the entry hall brought her to a halt. Through the doorway Jill saw Bennett pass by. He approached the front door, clad in the same tan-colored down jacket he had worn the previous morning when—after pocketing the cigarette lighter—he had slipped discreetly from the inn. In fact, his attire was the same as yesterday's, item for item: the same white overalls, blue work shirt, and brown hiking boots he had been wearing since their arrival at Moon's End.

Bennett opened the front door and stole outside. Jill wondered what business could possibly be taking him out there into the snow—

the second time in less than twenty-four hours she had asked herself that question. She went to the broad picture window and peered outside, but Bennett was already gone.

She felt lonely. Like when Daddy left. She had always wanted to be a detective, like Daddy, and truly earn his trademark praise of "Good girl, Jill." But she wanted to succeed on her own merits, not ride on his coattails. So she used her mom's maiden name of Constable rather than Templar.

To have stayed with Bryan would have meant betraying Daddy But then, five years later, she learned that Bryan had been right about Daddy all along. And when Mom found out, her health eroded further. No wonder Jill had ended up in Lakeview.

Jonas had visited her there during those two years. And then, when she was finally released, finding Jonas still waiting … She had lost Bryan *and* Daddy, and Mom's health was slipping away. It was a mistake, getting involved with Jonas, but she had needed comfort. At least for a while. Mom never met Jonas, but she knew Jill was seeing someone. She called him Jill's "young man."

When Jill had time to sort things out, she regretted her decisions. She decided to go to Bryan and try to make amends. Imagine her surprise to learn from the sign on the office door that Bryan and Jonas were partners. Jonas had never mentioned that. If Bryan found out about her and Jonas—his best friend … Well, she could not let that happen. She knew Jonas would keep their secret. But she also knew that Jonas was adamant about Bryan's unsuitability for her, and if she tried to resume a relationship with Bryan, Jonas would sabotage it to "protect" her, by telling Bryan about them.

So they had to stay apart.

As things worked out, she found a way—thanks to Imogen—to manage with Bryan out of her life. If only he had *stayed* out.

THE SNOW FELT cold beneath his feet. He could feel it penetrate his leather boots. But he had business to attend to.

Jill had seen him leave the inn, dressed in his white overalls, work shirt, and hiking boots. Of that he was certain. Would she say anything? Probably not. There would be no reason to. No one would come looking for him. For the time being, he was safe.

Except for the gun. That was a problem. How had it disappeared from Amanda's room? And who had it now?

Trying to upset him like that, when it had all been *their* doing: his fellow "guests." They were responsible. They thought they were all so smart, flaunting their wits at every opportunity, thinking, "Don't mind Bennett, the harmless fool." Little did they suspect …

One by one they were being destroyed, and where were their wits to save them now? He enjoyed watching their humiliating defeat.

He would be glad when they all were dead.

42

None of the guests were anxious to reassemble, preferring their own protected space defended by vigilance. For the rest of the morning and part of the afternoon the former classmates followed their own orbits, lost in a timeless world of heightened awareness. It was already midday when Bryan entered the billiard room, encountering Jonas at the pool table. A game of Eight Ball helped pass the time.

"I passed Amanda on my way in here." Bryan peered over his pool cue. "She seemed kind of moody."

"Well, it's not every day you kill someone unintentionally. That surprise visit by Reeve—"

"If it *was* a surprise." A third voice had uttered the remark. Neither man had noticed Hatter standing in the billiard room doorway. "*If* she hadn't been expecting it, that is."

Jonas missed his shot.

"Someone wanted Reeve to think the note he had received was an invitation from Amanda," Hatter continued. "How do we know it wasn't?"

"Awfully careless of her, don't you think," Bryan said, "not to have retrieved the note from Reeve's pocket before we arrived in her room?"

"Was it?" Hatter's spider-leg eyebrows contracted. "After all, what did you yourself conclude? That somebody *else* had sent it."

"Then how do you explain the attack on Amanda earlier?" Jonas asked.

"How do we know there *was* an attack? We have only Amanda's word for that. Did anyone actually see it happen?"

Jonas thought a moment. "You know, when I tried to get a closer look at her, she wouldn't let me near. At the time I gave it no thought—being typical behavior for Amanda—but maybe it was to conceal the fact that there *were* no marks on her neck."

"I thought you believed the killer to be a ghost, Hatter," Bryan said.

"I do. But you have to admit, it's an intriguing theory. After having worked on hundreds of murder cases, our prosecutor just may have come up with the perfect murder. She is 'assaulted'; so not only is she no longer a suspect, but she has all the more reason to shoot the 'intruder.' We could actually have seen her pull the trigger, and still no one would have suspected her. Instead, we would all be looking for an alleged 'assailant' who had attacked Amanda and sent Reeve the note."

Bryan offered Hatter the rare tribute of a surprised look. "You know something, Hatter, you might not be quite the fool I took you for. But there is still one problem with your theory. What's Amanda's motive?"

Silence.

"Actually," Jonas finally said, "*you* might have stumbled upon that, Hatter. Did you see the look on Amanda's face when you suggested she was connected to the warehouse fire?"

"How could she be connected?" Bryan protested. "It was Capaldi who set that fire."

"And when he did," Jonas explained, "the case Amanda had been building against him for years was destroyed overnight."

Bryan nodded. "It was a stroke of luck that police found that key at the warehouse. It allowed them to discover Capaldi's ledger and revive Amanda's case."

"And you think it was more than luck," Hatter said.

Jonas grinned. "I have sources working close to that case. They told me the key was sooty but uncharred when they found it."

"Which means," Bryan concluded, "it was planted *after* the fire."

Hatter watched his two companions closely. "You think Amanda planted it—to save her case."

"There's your motive, Hatter. If her evidence-planting came to light, it would mean the end of her career. And each of us was in a position to stumble upon the truth. Reeve worked for Capaldi. Bennett had an unsavory connection with him, too, as did Damien. Which Carter was apparently aware of."

"Reeve had 'confessed' some of those activities to Gideon," Hatter added. "Perhaps enough to jeopardize Amanda's secret."

"Jill is Amanda's friend," Bryan added. "Who knows how much she knew?"

"But what about me?" Hatter asked. "I wasn't in a position to know anything."

Purposeful footsteps in the hallway silenced the group as Amanda strode into the room, considering each man briefly.

"Jonas," she said slowly, "I need to talk to you. In private. I need to know ..."

The men's expressions stopped the words in her throat. Few etiquette books tell what to do when an accusation of murder is interrupted by the accused herself.

"You were talking about me, weren't you? I should have known. And I almost asked one of you to ..."

With a scowl, Amanda turned and stomped out the door.

"I thought you wanted to ask me something," Jonas called after her.

"Never mind. I'll work it out myself."

This time the men assured themselves of her absence before speaking.

"I wonder what she wanted?" Jonas asked. "It's not like Amanda to consult anyone."

Gideon appeared in the doorway. "Has anyone seen Bennett lately?"

No one had.

"I haven't seen him since this morning. I wonder where he's gone off to."

"Probably in his room."

"Do you think Bennett really knows who sabotaged the stunt that killed Julian Hayward?" Gideon asked.

"Let me ask you this," Jonas said. "If the stunt was sabotaged, *when* was it done? The day before the accident, after shooting was wrapped up, Amanda and I inspected the scaffolding, and there was nothing wrong with it. That evening, Damien staked out the set until—"

Gideon was impaled by their stares.

"Why don't you just say it?" he blurted out. "Everyone's been avoiding the subject since we arrived here."

"All right," Jonas began warily. "Damien was replaced by you, Gideon, and you kept watch until—"

"My accident," Gideon finished for him.

"As long as we've brought the subject out into the open," Bryan said, "I'd like to know exactly what happened that night. I never did get the full story, since I was pulled—" Bryan did not complete the sentence.

Gideon relived the nightmare from which he had never fully awakened. Late that night he had replaced Damien, keeping watch without incident until early morning, when an unusual noise drew him from his post, leading him through the dark over a large trap door, whose opener mechanism, they later discovered, had been tampered with. Gideon's weight on the platform forced it open, dropping him into a deep pit.

Gideon's cries for help summoned the night watchman. With a shriek of sirens, the paramedics arrived. By the time Gideon set off for the hospital, Hatter had already arrived on the lot to relieve him.

The scaffolding had thus been guarded without interruption since Jonas and Amanda had inspected it the previous evening.

"The only people who got near the scaffolding while I was on duty," Hatter insisted, "were the three construction workers who completed the work on it. After that, the filming began."

"Which brings up an interesting question," Jonas said. "How could the set have been sabotaged when no one had an opportunity to get near it?"

"Yet it *was* sabotage—rather than an accident—because the set was perfectly safe when you examined it," Gideon reminded Jonas.

"It's interesting how everything keeps coming back to that movie lot case," Bryan concluded.

Jill entered the room. "It's snowing," she announced.

Like curious children the group migrated to the parlor room windows.

"Where's Amanda?" Jill asked, noting her friend's absence.

"Here," Amanda called from the doorway. "I jüst came down for a bite to eat."

"Care to join us?"

"Not now. I'll eat in my room."

Her companions heard her mount the stairs. Eventually growing uncomfortable in one another's presence, they drifted to the far corners of the inn, as if awaiting the inevitable.

43

Amanda locked the door of her room, then glanced at the latch on the window: still pressed in. She sat at the writing desk, trying to marshal her unruly thoughts, but they ran riot.

What would she do, now that Reeve was dead? How could she get Imogen back? Amanda felt as helpless as she had felt as a teen working at Healing Heart, the receiving home for abused children. The horrible things she had seen there—battered, abused little girls, broken spirits, lives ruined by the age of five—had triggered at the time vague memories of her own childhood … things she told herself had not happened, things she did not want to remember, shameful things she had never told anyone.

Her years at Healing Heart had set her on the path of protecting defenseless children. She had devoted her entire adult life to stopping and punishing those who victimize others. She would rid the city of people who force innocent children into homes like Healing Heart. And to do so—effectively—she would need to become District Attorney.

Did she have what it takes to rise to the top? Of course. Look how she had outsmarted everyone up here. She knew they would never figure it out. It was her wits against theirs. And she was one step ahead. They had missed it. Only one thing remained to be worked out.

Something Jill had said …

A noise from behind interrupted her thoughts. Amanda turned to see what it was.

THROUGH THE PARLOR room's north door, an L-shaped corridor flanked by downstairs bedrooms culminated in the library, where Hatter stood examining the modest book collection lining walnut bookshelves.

He had been the first to stop watching the dwindling snowfall, to head off in search of reference material on the supernatural. For ideas for more punishments … for the characters in his new book. But all he had found were two collections of ghost stories and an outdated encyclopedia.

So they thought he was crazy. Let them. The supernatural passes sentence on all offenders, punishing crimes that can't be forgiven. Not only the crime of disbelief, but the crime of thumbing one's nose at Destiny. For a criminal, unlike a victim, *chooses* to commit an offense. Let them thumb their noses at that.

Because in the end, Hatter knew he would have the last laugh.

BRYAN KEPT AN eye on the doorway the entire time. If anyone came from the entry hall into the billiard room, he would know of it.

After Hatter had departed—for the library, presumably, since his bedroom was upstairs—Bryan had returned to the billiard room to relax and think. And to plan his next move. On a table top, he noticed the cassette recorder they had found during Friday's search of the inn and mountaintop. A cassette was in the recorder. Was the device still functional? He tested it. It still worked. Bryan pondered the possible advantage to which this could be put.

Sometimes everything you do only seems to make matters worse. Trying to avenge his parents had cost him Jill. His attempt to abandon the crusade against Paul Templar and reconcile with Jill had gotten him nowhere. And now the fiasco with Imogen. The more you try to fix something, the more harm you do. *Because it's not broken,* Dad would have said.

He should have seen the pattern foreshadowed fifteen years ago. Trying to solve the movie set case, only to be pulled off it by Damien, desperate to stop the director from pressing charges. If he had just given Bryan the files he had asked for, Bryan wouldn't have had to use that actress (what was her name?) to lure him out of his office while Bryan rifled the files. And if the set designer hadn't walked into the office right at that moment, no one would ever have known.

Bryan removed from his pocket the anonymous note that he had received last week. Who could have sent it? It had to have been one of the people here. Thank goodness his indiscretion had not been more widely publicized than among the trainees at Anderson's. If the State Licensing Board had gotten wind of it, he'd never have been granted a license. And they would pull that license from him in a heartbeat, if they ever found out.

There was something he had overlooked. What? He reviewed the entire weekend, from their arrival at Owen's Reef and conveyance here by Bill and Max to the murders that had ensued. Had they arrived only yesterday? It seemed like ages ago.

But it would be over soon.

JONAS SAT ALONE in the parlor room, staring at the copy of the birth certificate someone had sent him this week. A Mexican birth certificate. If anyone knew he was in this country illegally, they could have him sent back to Mexico.

Obviously, someone knew.

And the fact that this birth certificate had arrived at the same time as the invitation to the reunion strongly suggested that this person was one of his fellow guests. One of them was threatening to have Jonas deported.

And part of the reason Jonas was here was to find out which one.

Jonas looked obliquely across the hall to the entrance of the billiard room, to which Bryan had returned. Hatter had entered the north wing (bound presumably for the library). Amanda was in her room. Jonas did not know what had become of Bennett, Gideon, or Jill.

What had Amanda wanted to ask him? Had she discovered the murderer's identity?

What clues have been left behind? he wondered. *How would Bryan tackle the problem?* The thought escaped before could he suppress it. Should he ask Bryan? He and Bryan were incompatible opposites, with nothing in common. Bryan at least could show tangible signs of success; Jonas, less successful, was a failure.

Still, with so much at stake …

Jonas marched into the billiard room.

"I've been thinking about this game," he began. "The problem is lack of physical evidence. In terms of tangibles, what do we have? Only that cigarette lighter Bennett pocketed yesterday when we first arrived. But that has disappeared, which leaves us nothing. So let's consider intangibles."

Whatever response Jonas had been expecting, it was certainly not the one Bryan gave. "Why are you asking me, when someone else appears to know more than she's letting on?"

"Amanda?"

"Why not ask her what she knows?"

"Why not *both* ask her? We're supposed to die by tomorrow. What have we got to lose?"

In silent agreement, the men left the billiard room and ascended the stairs to Amanda's room.

Jonas rapped on the door.

No reply.

"Amanda … it's us, Jonas and Bryan."

Still no reply.

Jonas knocked harder and called louder.

"Amanda."

The door was unlocked. The men entered.

They found her lying on the floor beside the writing table.

44

Jonas turned Amanda's body over.

"Shot to death."

Bryan confirmed the death with an examination of the blood-soaked bullet hole in Amanda's blouse.

"Straight through the heart."

Bryan stood up and looked around the room. No sign of a struggle. An opened, half-eaten can of tuna sat on the writing desk, beside a fork. The window latch was pushed in all the way, in the locked position. But they had found the bedroom door unlocked. Amanda, defiant until the end, seemed to have thumbed her nose at danger with an unlocked door.

"It doesn't make sense," Jonas said. "She wouldn't have left her door unlocked, with a murderer on the loose."

"Maybe she didn't," Bryan suggested. "Maybe she locked her door, and then later let someone into the room."

"Knowing she could be letting in a killer?"

"Maybe it was someone she trusted."

The two men continued to examine the room in silence.

"She fell close to the writing desk," Bryan pointed out. "My guess is that she was standing there—with the door on the right side and window on the left—when her assailant shot her." Bryan passed a cold eye over the lifeless figure lying in a crumpled heap. "The position of the body makes it impossible to say where her killer was standing when he fired the shot."

"One thing we do know. She wasn't shot at close range. No powder burns."

"And then the killer simply waltzed out of the room, leaving the door unlocked."

A shadow fell across the corpse. Jill stood in the doorway.

"What happened? Is she—?"

Jonas nodded. "Shot to death. I'm sorry, Jill."

Jill sobbed. "But wouldn't we have heard a gunshot?" she finally asked.

"Apparently our killer came equipped with a silencer."

"Strange," Bryan muttered. "This murder seems … different … from the others. Hasty. Not as well-planned."

"What do you mean?"

"Someone is not just trying to kill us. He could have done so well before now. No, it's all a game. He's showing off his skill. But this is different. Too straightforward. Not ingenious, like the others. As if it had been improvised at the last moment."

Jill disappeared down the stairs to inform the others, leaving Bryan and Jonas to add Amanda's body to the frozen meat locker outside, beneath the newly fallen snow.

"So, who's your prime suspect?" Bryan asked as they dug.

"Well, Gideon seems to be out of it. Amanda was murdered upstairs in her room, and Gideon couldn't have gotten up the stairs. Nor could he have removed the guns from the furnace in the basement or attacked Amanda on the staircase last night. Or hidden Damien's body in the upstairs closet."

Bryan looked noncommittal. "What about Hatter?"

"A bit on the crazy side, but harmless enough, I think. Besides," Jonas continued, "he *was* almost one of the victims."

"I'm glad *someone* remembered that." Hatter stood in the doorway of the inn. "You have to be a dedicated murderer to kill yourself along with your other victims. After all, I could have died."

"But you didn't," Bryan observed meaningfully. "Interesting, isn't it? Carter died. You didn't. You'd think the killer would have given you both the same dose."

Hatter's eyes moved away from Bryan and Jonas toward the hole they had been digging. "What are you two doing out here?"

"Don't you know?" They stepped aside to reveal Amanda's body.

Hatter conducted his own postmortem. "Shot," he noted. "Just like Reeve."

Hatter lent a hand with the burial. Before returning inside, Bryan led the other two men in an apparently aimless circuit around the perimeter of the inn. Back inside the inn, the guests reassembled in the drawing room.

"I think the best approach is to try and reconstruct what happened," Gideon suggested.

The last time they had seen Amanda alive was when she had come down for something to eat while they were in the parlor room. As she returned to her room, the others had watched the snow fall for a while before dispersing to various parts of the inn.

"I was in the library the entire time," Hatter claimed.

"I can vouch for that," Jonas said. "I was in the parlor room. The only way out of the library is to go back through the downstairs corridor into the parlor room, and from there out into the entry hall to the stairs. Hatter couldn't have gone upstairs to Amanda's room without passing me in the parlor room."

Unless, Gideon suggested, the parlor room had been left vacant for a period of time. This Jonas vehemently denied, insisting that he had remained in the room as fixed as furniture, from the time Amanda had retired to her own room until just before he and Bryan discovered her body.

"What if Hatter went up to her room *after* you left the parlor room?" Gideon asked Jonas.

"He'd still have to have passed the billiard room," Bryan replied. "And I'd have seen him."

"Aren't we forgetting something?" Jill pointed out. "The library windows."

"They're picture windows. They don't open."

"True. But if a pane can be removed, Hatter could have left through those."

"We just checked outside," Bryan said. "There were no footprints in the snow outside those windows, or any of the inn's windows, for that matter. If Hatter had gone out a window, he'd have left footprints in the snow."

"Unless those footprints were covered by falling snow."

"It stopped snowing just before Hatter went into the library."

"So that gives Hatter an alibi," Jill concluded.

"It also gives you an alibi—of sorts—Jonas," Gideon added, "if you never left the parlor room. But—forgive me—how do we know it's true? How do we know *you* didn't kill Amanda?"

"I can answer that," Bryan interjected. Bryan had been in the billiard room the entire time, he said, with an eye fixed on the door to the entry hall. To get from the parlor room to the staircase, Jonas would have had to cross the entry hall past the billiard room—crossing Bryan's line of sight, as well.

"It's the same alibi," Hatter told Bryan, "with the same objection. It depends on the truth of your claim that you never left the billiard room. But we've no way of ascertaining that." A Hatter-like way of showing gratitude, rewarding Jonas' support of Hatter's alibi by undermining Jonas'. "Which means *you* could have murdered Amanda, Bryan. There's no proof that you didn't."

"Isn't there?" Jonas said. "From where I sat, I had a clear view of the door to the billiard room—a door Bryan had to go through to get to the staircase, if he wanted to murder Amanda. If he had left, I would have seen him. Besides, I could hear him playing billiards the entire time."

Jill connected the dots. "Then according to your stories, none of you could have gotten upstairs undetected. None of you could have murdered Amanda."

"Which leaves you and Gideon," Hatter concluded. "Where were you during this time period?"

"We were talking together here in the drawing room," Gideon answered quickly for the pair. "The entire time."

Jill nodded mute agreement.

"So you two provide each other with an alibi," Hatter reflected.

"All of us appear to have alibis," Bryan noted.

"Could Amanda have committed suicide?" suggested Gideon. "We have to consider all possibilities."

"Amanda was shot to death," Bryan replied. "Yet we didn't find a gun in her room—or outside. She was shot in the heart, and therefore died instantly. So how could she have gotten rid of the gun, if she was already dead? No, the shooter took that gun away with him. It wasn't suicide. It was murder."

"Not just murder," Jonas said. "We appear to have on our hands a murder that could not have been committed."

"An impossible murder," Hatter whispered, his face pale as moonlight. "I was right. It's a ghost."

"Remind me, Hatter," Bryan said. "Which ghost is it that's been killing us?"

"I've been giving that a lot of thought. With Amanda and Reeve's connection to Capaldi, it could be the warehouse foreman who died in that fire. He may have had some connection to Carter and Damien, as well."

"But the foreman had nothing to do with the rest of us."

"True. There's also that innocent bystander police shot in front of the psychic fair, who would certainly have a grudge against Bennett—and maybe you, too, Gideon, given your complicity in the theft. Apparently you, Bryan, and you, Jill, were there, too. But the spirit of the bystander would have no reason to go after the others. No, what we're looking for is someone with a common connection to all of us."

"And who would that be?"

"Damien."

"Damien," Jonas repeated. "We're being murdered by Damien's ghost?"

"Then who murdered Damien?" Bryan asked coyly.

Hatter shrugged. "Maybe one of us. Maybe not. That's precisely the point. Damien doesn't know who killed him. So he has to kill all of us, to cover his bases."

"I hate to throw cold water on this séance," Bryan interjected, "but isn't there one person we're forgetting?" His glance took in all of them. "Where's Bennett?"

"Of course," Jill said. "If none of us could have killed Amanda, it *had* to have been Bennett."

"So it would seem," Gideon agreed. "Yet I haven't seen him around since this morning."

Bryan and Jonas checked Bennett's room. He was not there.

"When was the last time anyone saw him?" Jonas asked.

"I saw him leave the inn," Jill replied. "But that was well before ten o'clock this morning." She consulted her wristwatch. "It's after four now."

Bryan's eyes narrowed. "He went outside?"

"It doesn't make sense," Gideon objected, "his disappearing like that. It's as good as a confession."

"Gideon has a point," Jill said. "Why would Bennett tip his hand like that?"

"That's something we're going to have to let Bennett explain for himself," Jonas replied. "After we find him. Wherever he is, he can't stay hidden long. Anyone coming with me?"

"I'll go." Bryan turned to Hatter and Jill. "You three stay here. Jill, you and Hatter—"

"What, Bryan? Protect me?" Bitterness contorted Gideon's face. "I may be confined to this wheelchair, but I assure you I can take care of myself."

"Obviously," Bryan said.

Gideon glared. "What's that supposed to mean?"

"Well, I was just wondering. You were caught by police 'assisting' Bennett in his theft of Capaldi's ledger. Surely you were locked up. Yet somehow you appear to have gotten yourself released."

"Bennett bailed me out," Gideon explained.

"Clearly, then, the police don't know that Bennett was your accomplice," Jonas reasoned. "Which means you're protecting him for some reason—after he left you holding the bag. What is Bennett holding over your head?"

"Nothing," Gideon insisted. "He just promised to help me."

Bryan eyed him shrewdly. "I think he promised to help you find the person who put you in that wheelchair."

"He said he had reason to believe it was one of the trainees," Gideon confessed. "He promised, if I kept his secret, to come to the reunion and help me find out which one."

"And you believed him?" Hatter asked.

"You don't know what it's like, any of you," Gideon cried. "To never even know why. Or who ..."

Gideon spun his chair around and wheeled himself powerfully from the drawing room.

"That was dramatic," Bryan remarked. "However, I think Gideon's not as vulnerable as he pretends to be."

"Obviously," Jill observed, "he feels vulnerable enough to be uncomfortable staying alone with two people, either of whom could be the murderer, while you two go off in search of Bennett. Clearly he feels safer locked in his room."

"He won't be safe there," Hatter predicted.

Bryan and Jonas disappeared to retrieve heavy coats and gloves from their rooms, leaving Jill alone with Hatter.

"I overheard you and Bryan talking this morning," Hatter said, "as well as Bryan talking to Gideon and Bennett. Apparently Bennett stole some evidence from the police and hid the key to the evidence locker in your daughter's pocket. Tell me, Jill, what was a five-year-old girl doing wandering unattended in front of a psychic fair?"

"Not that it's any business of yours," Jill replied, "but the fair was held right next door to the police station and welfare office—"

"I know. I was a speaker there, remember?"

"I had a meeting at the welfare office. I left Imogen alone in the waiting room, just for a few minutes."

"A protective parent."

"Thanks, Hatter. Just what I needed to hear. But there were certain things I didn't want her saying to the welfare people. I told her to stay put, but through the window she saw all of those people attending the fair in their exotic costumes, and the lure was too much for her. She wandered outside to see."

"Just as Bennett was fleeing from the police station. Talk about bad timing."

Bryan and Jonas returned, wearing coats and gloves.

"You two be careful," Jonas told Hatter and Jill, "in case Bennett returns."

Before leaving, Bryan asked Jill, "How was Bennett dressed when you saw him leave?"

"He was still wearing his work shirt and those white overalls." She added, as an afterthought, "And the tan-colored down jacket he was wearing yesterday afternoon."

"Not camouflaged," Jonas said. "This should be easy."

Bryan did not look as convinced.

46

GIDEON UNLOCKED THE door to his room and wheeled himself inside, locking the door after him. The window latch was still pressed in, locked. On the writing table sat the open juice can he had sealed in the room. He guzzled what remained in the can. Warm, but he didn't care.

It had been an exhausting day. His body melted into the wheelchair.

It was just before he fell asleep that the unwanted thoughts came. The people here were not to blame for his condition. They had done nothing. And yet *someone* had tampered with that trap door.

Gideon unthinkingly reached for … Where was the crucifix normally dangling from his neck? That's right, the jeweler was repairing a break in one of the chain's weaker links. It was not God who had pulled that lever, but a human being. God's fairness must never be questioned.

Gideon felt woozy. Perhaps the stress of the weekend? All of a sudden, he could barely keep his eyes open. *Stay alert, Gideon. You've got enemies out there.*

He shouldn't be bitter. He had survived. Four people dead so far, but he was still alive.

For years he had wondered who it had been—who had sabotaged that trap door. Until he knew who was responsible, he would have to blame everyone. It was not a matter of revenge. There would simply be no peace until he could finally put it to rest, settle the matter once and for all.

Until that time, the only repose he knew was in the serene oblivion of sleep.

THE RECENTLY FALLEN snow swaddled the mountaintop. For the moment, nature favored Bennett by effacing his footprints. If not for the fresh snowfall, finding him would have been as simple as following his tracks. Now method would have to replace luck, starting with a search of the garage and work shed.

Both were empty, yet something in the work shed was not the same. An item was missing. Everything seemed to be in its place: the tools in their racks, the extension ladder still hanging on the wall, the garden hose coiled in the corner. And then Jonas realized what it was. The work shed shovel had disappeared.

"Why would Bennett do it?" Jonas asked as they combed the mountaintop. "Why murder his former classmates? Revenge for a handful of pranks at his expense fifteen years ago?"

"I think it might be more serious than that. As that note he received implied, all of us were in a position to expose his theft of Capaldi's ledger to the police. Gideon was his accomplice. Jill and I were actually there, with Hatter nearby. Reeve worked for Capaldi, and Damien was on his payroll, as well. He didn't know if Carter was in on it with Damien. Amanda was investigating Capaldi, as were you and I."

"So he had to silence us all, to protect himself?"

"So it seems."

Despite the lack of footprints, the odds frowned on Bennett's chance of winning a game of hide-and-seek on a mountaintop offering no hiding places. His pursuers had passed through a cluster of narrow-trunked trees when Jonas stopped and stared across a clearing.

"What is it?" Bryan asked.

"I'm not sure." Jonas pointed. "Over there."

"Looks like some kind of marker. Whatever it is, it wasn't there when we searched the area yesterday."

The men's approach brought the object into sharper focus: the missing shovel from the work shed, its head buried in the snow.

Seizing the shovel, Jonas began to dig for answers.

"There's something down there."

"Bring it up."

Like a sculptor, Jonas chipped away at the ice and snow to free the image trapped within.

It was Bennett.

"He's been here for some time," Jonas observed. "Long enough to have gotten this cold."

"Which makes it impossible to tell exactly *how* long."

"A good many hours, at least. He was probably murdered shortly after Jill saw him leave the inn this morning."

"When everyone was on their own—leaving the murderer free to slip out of the inn, murder Bennett, and return unnoticed. Which means it could have been anyone."

The men scoured the corpse with expert eyes. Unquestionably Bennett was dead; yet his unbruised limbs betrayed no sign of a struggle. The only evidence of violence was a large stain of congealed blood discoloring Bennett's work shirt around the deep knife wound in his chest. Spurts of blood tarnished his tan down jacket as well, but his unsoiled white pants had been spared blemish of any kind. The men examined the chest wound.

"Stabbed through the heart," Jonas noted.

"This is the first murder to have taken place away from the inn," Bryan mused. "I wonder why."

"Greater privacy? No one around to witness the murder."

"True. But at the same time, there's greater risk—that the murderer's absence from the inn might be noticed—and his identity thus given away. The murderer took a big chance coming here. What made him so certain he could get away with it? One would think the risk—of exposure—to have outweighed the advantages. And this killer is not one who takes chances."

"Which brings up another question. What was Bennett doing out here?"

"It seems unlikely that Bennett would wander this far for no reason."

"Not with a killer on the loose," Jonas agreed. "Which means that the murderer must have arranged with Bennett to meet here. But under what kind of pretext, I wonder?"

"Especially when Bennett must have been suspicious of any arrangement as questionable as a private meeting in an isolated place outside the inn. When he knew one of us is a murderer."

"And then there's the question of how Bennett could have been taken so completely by surprise—without even putting up a fight—when he should have been on his guard, knowing that at least three other murders had already been committed."

They examined the body further, with an unexpected result. From the left front pocket of Bennett's overalls Jonas withdrew a small object.

"The cigarette lighter," he exclaimed. "The one we gave Bennett—thinking he was Aaron the caretaker—when we first arrived here."

"The one he later denied having."

"Was he lying? Did he have it the entire time?"

"When we asked him about the lighter, he truly seemed puzzled."

"Besides, what would he be trying to conceal by lying? Clearly he's not the murderer."

"And anyway, Reeve searched him, remember? And didn't find the lighter."

"Could he have missed it?"

Both men dismissed the likelihood.

The corners of Bryan's eyes crinkled. "Which leaves us the alternative explanation. Someone, undoubtedly the murderer, stole the lighter from him. Why? Because it provides a clue to the killer's identity? If so, why did he return it to Bennett—to the very pocket from which it had been taken?"

"To get rid of the evidence?" Jonas suggested. "Bury it with Bennett?"

"And then mark the grave?" Bryan's eyes stole down to Jonas' hand. "Let's have a look at that cigarette lighter."

The lighter was an ordinary silver model, in working condition. No monogram, no unusual markings of any kind. Nor any out-of-the-ordinary signs of wear. Nothing, in fact, that could be construed as a clue, nor anything that pointed to its owner's identity.

They decided to leave Bennett's body where it was, re-covering the hole with snow.

"It seems obvious," Bryan said, "that our killer planted this shovel because he wanted us to find Bennett's body."

"Then why did he kill Bennett way out here—*and bury him*? There was no guarantee that anyone would see Bennett leave the inn—and burying him would certainly not increase our odds of finding him. If the killer wanted us to find Bennett's body, why not just leave it out here *on* the snow, for us to find? By burying it, the murderer was taking a chance that no one would discover the body at all."

"Of course," Bryan said, "he could have been trying to conceal the murder; but then, if he did *not* want the body to be found, why mark the grave?"

Which left them with more questions than answers. Never before had they been so baffled.

But things were to become more baffling yet.

"WHAT HAVE YOU got there?" Bryan asked as he and Jonas returned to the inn.

"The murderer's second note," Jonas replied. "Listen: '... the next victim has already been chosen. In fact, I have a special surprise in store for him: one he'll never guess, though I'm sure he'll take a stab at it.' Anything strike you about those lines?"

"Aside from the dreadful melodrama?"

"Be serious, Bryan. It sounds to me like our killer was saying that the next victim would be *male*. Note the repetition of 'he' and 'him.' But the victim we found after this note was Amanda."

"Read it to me again." Jonas obliged. "Yes, he was referring to Bennett. Even the phrase 'take a stab at it' hints at the method he intended to use."

"If Bennett, rather than Amanda, was intended as the next victim, then—"

"The victims were killed—or at least discovered—out of order."

"Which means that the murderer killed Amanda sooner than he had planned to," Jonas concluded. "Why?"

"Remember when Amanda wanted to talk to you but didn't? I think she knew something, or was working something out. And the murderer knew it. He had to eliminate her before she could pass her knowledge on to anyone else. Hence, she was murdered ahead of schedule." Bryan stopped walking. "I *thought* there was something wrong about her murder. It just seemed too rushed."

Bennett, they had concluded, had to have been murdered and buried in the snow that morning, for him to have been as cold as he was when they discovered him. That very fact, unfortunately, made it impossible to determine how long he had been buried. And therefore to pinpoint the exact time of death.

Which made the question of alibis academic—for Bennett's murder. But not for Amanda's.

Everyone had an alibi for Amanda's murder. Everyone except Bennett. But Bennett had clearly been killed in the morning, Amanda in the afternoon. Bennett could not have murdered her, for he was already dead by then. So who had?

"It wasn't suicide," Jonas argued, "with no gun found in her room. Yet according to what we know, no one could have killed her. Makes you want to reconsider Hatter's ghost theory, doesn't it?"

Bryan frowned. "There's only one alternative. Someone's alibi is vulnerable."

Hatter had been in the library, Jonas in the parlor room, and Bryan in the billiard room. Gideon and Jill had been together in the drawing room. Something had been overlooked …

"You corroborated Hatter's alibi," Bryan said. "You and I substantiate each other's. As for Gideon and Jill, we have only their word for it that they were together in the drawing room. No one actually saw them there."

"But to lie for someone—"

"Unless they're in on it together."

Jonas nodded. "That *has* to be how it was done. So we know one of them is the murderer. But Gideon could not have climbed the stairs to kill Amanda." An imperceptible pause. "Which leaves Jill."

But Bryan seemed reserved. "The first rule Damien taught us was to question every assumption. For instance: How do we *know* that Gideon does not have the use of his legs?"

"We know for a fact he fell and damaged his spine."

"Ah, but to what extent? And to what extent has he recovered in fifteen years?"

"So his wheelchair provides him with the perfect alibi. He couldn't have attacked Amanda on the staircase last night. He couldn't have stolen the guns from the basement. He couldn't have hidden Damien's body in the upstairs closet. And he couldn't have killed Amanda this afternoon." Jonas' eyes glistened in the fading twilight. "Or could he?"

"But why murder everyone? Unless … unless he blames us for his accident, and whatever damage he actually suffered. And wants revenge."

"Gideon never knew who tampered with that trap door. And then suddenly Bennett comes along and tells him it may have been one of us. Only he doesn't say which one. The only way for certain to repay the culprit would be—"

"To kill us all."

48

THEY FOUND HATTER in the entry hall, carrying a sealed jar of olives. "Any luck?" he asked indifferently as he led them into the parlor room, where he settled, removing a pad and pen from his pocket.

"Depends on how you mean it."

"You found Bennett, didn't you?" Hatter spoke with the arcane fatalism of a Delphic priest interpreting an omen. "And he was dead."

Resisting an urge to ask Hatter how he knew, Jonas merely said, "Stabbed through the heart."

"Like Damien," Hatter replied without emotion.

"Where are Gideon and Jill?" Bryan asked.

"Gideon is still in his room, I presume. I haven't seen Jill lately."

Hatter's pen hovered like a hawk over his notepad.

"Something wrong, Hatter?" Jonas asked.

Hatter passed a hand over a dark fringe of thinning hair vaulting hollow gray eyes set deep in a skeletal face. "Four down, five to go."

"A cheery thought."

"When are you going to face the facts, Bryan?" Hatter cried. "We're all going to die."

"But why, Hatter, why? Why would anyone want to kill us all? What's the motive?"

"The motive," Hatter said flatly, "is revenge."

"Yes, but revenge for what? Don't you see that if we only knew the motive, that in itself might point to the murderer?"

Jonas seemed jolted by a sudden thought. "You know, Bryan, we've been assuming from the start that someone wants to kill us all."

"The fact that we're all being murdered one by one does tend to support that view."

"But what if it doesn't? What if that is merely subtle misdirection? What if you just hit the nail on the head? You said that if we knew the motive, that in itself might point to the murderer." Jonas paused, arranging his thoughts. "Suppose you wanted to kill someone. You have a motive. But that motive points directly to you. If you murder your victim, everyone will know you had reason to do so. You will become the prime suspect. So what do you do?"

Bryan understood. "You conceal that motive by murdering a *group* of people. No one knows the *true* victim—or, therefore, the real motive."

The theory provoked a burst of derision from Hatter. "Are you saying that your murderer really wants to kill only *one* of us, and is murdering the others to camouflage his motive?"

"A motive which, if known, would point straight to the culprit."

But Hatter remained antagonistic. "Even if your theory is correct, it doesn't bring us any closer to the truth, because it doesn't answer two vital questions. Who is the intended victim, and who has a motive to kill him?"

Into the drawing room walked Jill. "Did you find Bennett?" she asked.

They related their discovery of Bennett's body.

"Who's next?" Jill whimpered. Suspicion ricocheted from eye to eye. "Wait a minute. When was Bennett killed?"

"This morning," Jonas replied.

"We were even warned—" Bryan began.

Jill interrupted. "What are you talking about?"

Jonas handed her the murderer's second note. "I'd love to compare this to the first note."

"I have it. It's in my room." Jill turned to leave.

"Wait," Bryan said. "Have you seen Gideon lately?"

"Not since you two left."

Bryan and Jonas exchanged concerned glances. As Jill returned to her room, the two former partners hastened toward Gideon's.

"Gideon?" Jonas called loudly, knocking on Gideon's door.

No reply. He pounded on the door. "Gideon, are you in there?" he shouted.

Still no response. Jonas eased the door open as Hatter arrived. No one wanted to enter alone, so all three entered together.

Gideon sat motionless in his wheelchair, peaceful as a sleeping infant.

"Gideon?" Jonas said softly. But nothing he did could wake Gideon from this sleep. Jonas searched for a pulse, or signs of breathing.

"He's not asleep," Jonas declared. "He's dead."

JILL STOOD IN the doorway, breathless.

"I heard shouting … I raced out of my room …" She noticed Gideon's lifeless form. "Oh, no, is he …"

Jonas lowered his eyes, while Hatter and Bryan examined the body to confirm Gideon's death. Though they found no signs of life, neither did they find signs of violence: no wounds, bruises, or marks of any kind.

"Neither shot nor stabbed," Bryan said. "No contusions on the skull, so we can rule out a blow to the head. Plus, he shows no consistent signs of poisoning, that I can discern. In my opinion, he was suffocated."

"Yes," Jonas agreed. "There are no marks around his throat, so strangulation is out. But notice the blue tinge to his lips and ears, and under his fingernails. Cyanosis: an excess of carbon dioxide when it is prevented from leaving the body. I think someone put a pillow to his face and smothered him."

Jill wore a puzzled expression. "The window is locked, but didn't you find the door unlocked?"

Hatter nodded. "Gideon was more careful than that. He would have locked the door."

"Then how did the murderer get in?"

"There's no way Gideon would have let someone into his room."

"Especially after Amanda was murdered in hers."

"Then how—?"

"I told you," Hatter said. "This murderer can do things others can't."

"Cut it out, Hatter. Things are already spooky enough without your help."

"Besides, if your spook entered the room through supernatural means, why didn't it leave that way? Instead, after murdering Gideon, the killer appears to have opened the door, passed through, and left the door unlocked. Just as he did with Amanda."

Jonas was staring at the corpse.

"What, Jonas?" Bryan asked.

"We agree that Gideon was suffocated. But there's no sign of a struggle. Which is not what one might expect of suffocation."

"Unless Gideon fell asleep in his wheelchair."

"If he was up all night like I was," Jill said, "he might have been tired enough to."

"Or he had help," Bryan said, pointing to the empty juice can. "If the murderer drugged that drink—"

"Then Gideon would have slept through anything," Jonas concluded. "So it would have been a simple matter to enter the room without waking him."

"Assuming the door was unlocked," Jill added.

"And it wouldn't have taken much strength to suffocate him, either," Hatter said. "Being drugged, he would have offered no resistance. Even a woman could have done it."

"Are you changing your mind about the killer being supernatural, Hatter?"

"Just stating possibilities."

"While we're listing possibilities," Bryan said to Hatter, "where were *you* while we were out looking for Bennett?"

In his bedroom the entire time, Hatter claimed, working on his book, until hunger drove him into the kitchen. Jonas noticed, however, that the notes scribbled across Hatter's small writing pad barely covered one entire page.

"So now it's down to us four …" Jill said.

"On the bright side," Jonas noted, "that makes the killer's job much more difficult. The narrower the list of suspects, the harder it becomes to kill undetected, since we have fewer people to keep an eye on. The murderer will have to be pretty clever to surprise three people on the lookout."

"Shouldn't we do something with Gideon?" Jill asked.

Hatter and Jonas carried the corpse outside, burying Gideon in a frozen bed beneath a blanket of snow. Bryan remained behind with Jill.

"You didn't ask me where *I* was this afternoon," Jill said. "But then, you also chose to stay behind just now."

"I wanted to ask you privately."

After Bryan and Jonas had left the inn, Jill explained, she preferred the risk of a quick, painless death at the hands of a murderer to the certainty of lingering torment in the company of Hatter, so she locked herself in her room until she heard the voices of the returning men.

"You don't think *I* murdered Gideon, do you?"

Bryan averted his eyes. "I don't know what to think."

"You know me better than that."

"It's been fifteen years."

"You knew me once."

"Did I? I'm not so sure. There was always a part of you that you seemed to be holding back."

"Look who's talking. The moment we broke up, you took up with that cheap actress. What was that, your idea of a birthday present?"

"I was hurt, Jill. And I was only using her to help me get to the director's files. Besides," he added, "I see *you* weren't too hurt to find someone else."

"What do you mean?" Jill struggled to control her panic. "Are you talking about Imogen?" A nervous laugh. "She's not my daughter, silly. Not my biological daughter, at least. She's Amanda's baby."

Bryan seemed lost for words.

"You were right about my father, Bryan. Eventually Mom and I found out. I couldn't handle it, on top of everything else. I spent two years in Lakeview—"

"I'm sorry, Jill."

"It was shortly after Dad left. Mom's health had never been great. The stress—of Dad, and my commitment—took its toll. Eventually Mom was hospitalized—cerebral hemorrhage. After Mom came home, Amanda gave birth to Imogen. It's a long story, Bryan, but I offered to raise her. Then Mom took a turn for the worse. It wiped me out financially. I had to go on welfare. Which meant lying about Imogen."

"You could have adopted her—"

"Not without bringing Amanda into it. I told you, it was complicated. But it was all working out—until you interfered. And now she's gone—"

Jill fled from the room as Hatter and Jonas returned.

"Looks like someone still blames you for the breakup years ago," Hatter taunted. "And from what I just heard, losing her daughter. She seemed angry enough to kill."

"You know, Hatter, for someone who believes the killer to be a ghost, you certainly are free with your accusations."

"Besides," Jonas added, "she has no motive to kill the rest of us."

Hatter pounced on Jonas' words. "Wasn't it you, Jonas, who had a theory about that? Let's say for a moment that Jill did want to kill Bryan. If she were to do so, an investigation of Bryan's past would lead directly to her. *He* was responsible for their breakup. *He* was responsible for the loss of her daughter. Two perfect motives. She would be the prime suspect. The only way to kill him without arousing suspicion would be to make it look like he was simply one of a group of victims. A search would be made for someone with a motive to kill everyone—which Jill doesn't have—rather than a motive to kill Bryan specifically."

"I see you're not as insistent on the ghost theory," Bryan observed, "when you are the only alternative to Jill as Gideon's murderer. You claim you were in your bedroom the entire time. Jill says she was in hers. Either of you could have entered Gideon's room and smothered him without alerting the other."

"But that doesn't explain Amanda's murder, does it?" Hatter snapped. "You said so yourself: None of us could have done it. There's only one explanation for that. And it's eventually going to get you, too."

"And you," Bryan pointed out.

Bryan's reminder sent Hatter retreating from the room.

"When we went off in search of Bennett," Bryan said half to himself, "we left Gideon alive. While we were gone, somebody murdered him."

"And that someone had to have been one of two people. Hatter or Jill."

"But Hatter's right. We still have to confront a different problem. Who killed Amanda?"

"We know it wasn't Bennett. And Hatter has an alibi—as do you and I. So it was either Gideon or Jill. And Gideon would seem to be exonerated."

Somehow, they reasoned, Jill had persuaded Gideon to supply her with an alibi. How this had failed to arouse Gideon's suspicion, neither man could fathom. Murdering Amanda under the cover of a vulnerable alibi, Jill then went about silencing Gideon, snipping off the one loose thread in her tightly woven scheme, the only one who could unravel that alibi.

"So what are we going to do now?"

"We keep an eye on her. We don't let her out of our sight. We only have to make it through one more night. Tomorrow Bill and Max return for us, and when they see the bridge is out, they'll send for help. Once we're rescued, we can decide what to do."

As Bryan removed a cigarette packet from his pocket, a flutter caught Jonas' eye. Something had fallen from Bryan's pocket. It lay on the floor beside his right foot, small and white. Whatever it was, Bryan had not noticed it fall.

"You look concerned," Bryan observed. "Perhaps rightly so. After all, Jill *was* in an asylum for two years. Who knows what she's capable of?"

When Bryan departed, Jonas scooped up the white object from the floor. A piece of paper, folded. Jonas unfolded the note and read it.

50

Eventually the four survivors were drawn like helpless pieces of metal to some magnetic center of doom, pulled by the force of a single issue: the best way to stay safe.

"We're not safe," Hatter whined, "together or apart."

"Hatter has a point," Jonas said. "Amanda and Gideon were locked in their rooms, and that didn't protect them."

Jill shook her head vigorously. "I'd still feel safer with locked doors between us."

"Locked doors can't keep this killer out," Hatter replied.

"Our strength is in numbers, Jill," Jonas said. "It's still three against one."

"The one has already gotten five of us," Hatter pointed out. "Plus Damien."

Jill glanced from person to person. "By not trusting one another, we're more likely to kill one another, like Amanda did to Reeve, and save the murderer the trouble."

"Maybe," Hatter suggested, "that's what he's counting on."

Jill stood up. "I'm sorry, but I feel safer looking after myself."

"Jill …" Jonas began, but Jill was already out of the drawing room.

"I'm with Jill," Hatter said.

Before Bryan and Jonas could speak, Hatter was as far beyond the threshold as he was beyond the reach of reason.

"So now what?" Jonas asked Bryan. "Do we stand guard in the corridors?"

"And guard whom? Jill? Hatter? Or split up and guard both?"

"What difference does it make? The murderer has the only guns. If Jill or Hatter comes out with a weapon, what are we going to do?"

"We'd be safer in our rooms," Bryan agreed.

"It's either all together, or everyone apart. And Hatter and Jill appear to have made that decision for us."

"Still, I don't like it," Bryan said as he left his ex-partner alone in the drawing room.

Jonas removed from his pocket the slip of paper Bryan had dropped earlier that evening. Once again he read the words typed on it:

> *Breaking into a director's office and stealing files is a misdemeanor. If the State Licensing Board found out, what would happen to your investigator's license? But how would they find out? Who would know about something that happened fifteen years ago?*

JILL SWALLOWED A CLONAZEPAM pill from the bottle on the end table beside her bed. She needed to relax, calm her nerves. One more night, and then everything would be behind her. She locked the door to her room. It was unfortunate, of course, the others dying. Especially Amanda. But her main concern now was her own safety.

She had to stay awake. She reached for the alarm clock. She would set it, to wake her in case she fell asleep. No, she was too worked up to fall asleep. No need to worry on that account.

She had to get Imogen back. Imogen needed her. Always had. Of course, taking in Imogen hadn't been entirely altruistic. Perhaps, in its way, it had been an act of desperation. One that had opened the floodgates of emotion.

You take care of your family. You protect the ones you love. You don't let anything stand in your way. Even when it means lying to the welfare office to protect Imogen. Or stealing pills from the nursing care facility, when Mom kept receiving the wrong medication. But even with all that, Mom's heart eventually gave out, and Imogen was taken away. Somehow Jill had to make things right, even if Bryan had to—

Suddenly Jill's limbs felt heavy. Her head began to feel fuzzy. *No, stay awake.* Only one day remained. One day to fix things.

THEY WERE CROSSING a suspension bridge over the ravine, Jill and he, escaping the deadly mountain peak to freedom. On the other side stood a dark, shadowy figure whose features Jonas could not discern. Beside the stranger sat an old-fashioned box-and-plunger detonator, the type used by caricature villains in the old westerns. The spectral figure depressed the plunger. An explosion snapped the ropes. The bridge unraveled at the far end and began to fall in slow motion …

Jonas awoke fitfully. He had dozed off, dreaming about that same bridge that had been haunting his thoughts for the last two days.

And not only *his* thoughts, apparently. Shortly before retiring for the evening, Bryan had stood before the fireplace mantle, staring at the detonator box they had found near the bridge. Yesterday the wooden box had intrigued Bryan; this evening it seemed to puzzle him. Yesterday Jonas had quipped about how well the dried-up piece of balsa would burn as firewood. Tonight he wondered what aspect of the detonator box could have accounted for Bryan's sullen silence.

The life of a farm worker was as stifling as a stagnant pond; but Jonas had to be a river, going somewhere. *What is wrong with where you are?* Papa would ask. He meant well, but he was naive. *If you're unhappy with your job, tell your boss.* And how would that have looked? Got to keep up appearances. Success and failure are incompatible. You can't be good if someone is better. Only the best are good.

And up here, trapped on this mountaintop with no possibility of escape, the best would be the one who survived.

51

BRYAN'S EYELIDS RESISTED the pull of gravity. There was too much that needed to be done. Too much that needed to be worked out. All of the signs had pointed in one direction; and then, suddenly, a dead end.

There were so many unanswered questions. Like the cigarette lighter they had found on Bennett when they had discovered his body. The lighter he had claimed to have lost. Had he been lying? How could having that lighter have possibly incriminated Bennett, who was clearly not the murderer, in any case?

Then why lie about it? Or had someone stolen it? Why then was it subsequently returned to Bennett's pocket?

It was curious how Bennett had been so easily taken by surprise, out in the open in broad daylight. What had he been thinking, going out there with a murderer on the loose?

And where had Bennett gone Friday afternoon, leaving the inn so soon after their arrival? Not the second time, when he went outside to emit the scream that drew them all from the inn, but the first time.

Bryan shook his head sleepily. His groggy mind was leaping from thought to thought, like a frog between two hotplates.

How had Jill known about that actress? He thought he had been so discreet. Jonas, of course, had known. Bryan had made the mistake of confiding in him the fact—which Bryan had found cruelly amusing at the time—that his affair with the actress (what was her name?) had commenced on, of all days, Jill's birthday. What had he been thinking? Had he really expected Jonas to respond with anything but icy disapproval? At least Bryan had had the sense to share the ironic fact with no one else.

He had been so impulsive in those days. How could he have been so young and naive, trying to steal the information the director had refused to share? He could lose his license if the State Board ever found out.

He had been reckless … young and reckless. He had allowed his passion for vengeance to take control. You try to untie a knot, and it becomes more tangled.

That was where it all began, on that movie set. *Nine Man Morris* … Nine Man's Murder. What was the connection? What had that graduation assignment to do with their current predicament? That was the key. And only one of them knew the answer.

The stunt accidents. The sabotaged scaffolding. Julian Hayward's unexpected substitution for Adam Burke on the deadly stunt when Burke twisted his ankle at the last moment. Julian's fatal fall. William Hayward's subsequent nervous breakdown and commitment to a mental institution. William and Amanda in the director's office on the morning of the accident, when one of the three construction workers completing work on the scaffolding called in sick.

We were all partly responsible for Julian Hayward's death, Bryan reflected. *Each of us contributed in his own way. Bunglers.*

Eight against one, and the eight were being picked off one by one. Bryan wouldn't be surprised if there was indeed only one left by morning.

HATTER'S REFLECTION WAS laughing at him. The public knew only Hatter Cates, the author—not Lawrence Cates, the person. It was the image who was famous. The person was still anonymous. So had he really fulfilled his destiny?

The muffled echo of commotion startled Hatter to his senses. Despite his efforts to stay awake, he had nodded off.

Drowsily Hatter consulted his wristwatch. Just past two o'clock. Who had set their alarm for two o'clock in the morning? And why did they not shut it off? Someone was a much sounder sleeper than Hatter.

Draping a warm robe over his clothes, he drifted downstairs.

Bryan was racing from his room to join Jonas before the closed door of Jill's bedroom. "I fell asleep," he said. "What's going on?"

As Hatter approached, the alarm grew quite loud, clanging behind Jill's door. Jonas knocked even louder.

"Jill, are you all right?"

No response.

"Jill, answer me."

He tried turning the doorknob. Locked. Bryan had no greater success.

"Something's wrong. We've got to get in there."

"How?"

Jonas was the first to come up with an idea. He disappeared down the hallway.

Hatter followed Jonas, leaving Bryan alone in the hallway outside Jill's bedroom door.

Hatter found Jonas in the service porch searching the storage closet. At length Jonas withdrew the object he sought: a large ax for cutting firewood.

The two men hurried back to Jill's bedroom, where Jonas, after one last futile attempt to turn the doorknob, hacked a hole in the door. Reaching inside, he found the lock on the doorknob that secured the bedroom door from within. Twisting it, he unfroze the doorknob. With a turn of the knob, he opened the door.

The clock alarm was still screaming for attention when the men entered the room. Jill was lying face down on the bed, in rumpled clothing on top of the blankets, hair sprawled like snakes in a fumigated vipers' nest.

They knew that the alarm could sound forever, but it would never wake the girl.

52

ON THE PILLOW beside Jill's head lay a small slip of paper. Jonas picked it up. On it were typed four words:

NOTHING CAN STOP ME.

As Jonas turned off the alarm, Bryan passed what he hoped was a cold, clinical eye over Jill's body. Jonas and Hatter confirmed her death. There was no sign of struggle, yet her crumpled clothing showed signs of unnecessary violence. All three men noticed the deep red indentation on her neck. Apparently she had been strangled with a rope or cord—

"Or bathrobe sash, perhaps."

"Could it have been suicide?" Hatter asked hastily.

Jonas sneered. "You can't strangle yourself to death. You'd pass out before you could finish the job. Besides, even if you could, Jill was strangled with a sash or cord. If she died at her own hands, how did she get rid of the cord after she died?"

For there was none in the room to be seen.

The three men looked over every inch of Jill's room that might conceal some clue. But the mockingly silent milk chocolate walls, broken only by the darker sepia of the closed closet door, presented a monotony of solid brown, unrelieved by even one window. Bryan and Jonas examined the lock on the inside knob of Jill's bedroom door. On the night table beside the bed was Jill's room key, next to a bottle of pills and a water bottle. They tested the key: It locked and unlocked Jill's door.

"No sign of a struggle," Bryan observed. "Jill was on her guard, like the rest of us. Yet the murderer appears to have taken her by surprise, strangling her without a fight."

Jonas approached the night table, scooped up the pill bottle, and read the label. "Unless she couldn't offer one. Clonazepam. A tranquilizer. Probably prescribed by some doctor at Lakeview." He set the bottle down. "If she took one or more pills tonight, she may have sedated herself to the point where she could offer no resistance."

Bryan joined Jonas at the night table. "But Jill wanted to stay awake and alert. If her pills normally made her sleepy, she wouldn't have taken any." Bryan picked up and opened the bottle. "However, if the murderer somehow replaced Jill's medication with sleeping pills, Jill might have taken a pill she *thought* would not put her to sleep."

"But what about the alarm clock?" Hatter asked.

"She might have set it to wake her up in case she *did* fall asleep," suggested Jonas.

"Or," Bryan said, "it was the murderer who set it, because he wanted us to find the body now. But how did he get in?" Bryan looked around the windowless bedroom. "There's only one way into this room: the door. And it was locked from within when we arrived."

"How do we know that it was locked earlier?" Hatter asked. "The killer could have come in through the unlocked door, strangled Jill—"

"And how did he lock the door when he left? If you turn the lock on the inside doorknob while the door is open, the knob freezes and you can't close the door. If you turn it with the door closed, you can't open the door to get out."

"But you can lock it from the outside with a key."

"We found the key on the night table, inside the room."

"And we know these keys weren't duplicated."

"Maybe," Hatter suggested, "the murderer killed Jill, took the key, used it to lock the door from the outside, and returned the key to the night table when we entered the room."

But all agreed that they had seen the key on the table upon entering the room, before anyone got within arm's reach of it. And no one had had an opportunity to swap it with a look-alike, even when they were testing it in her lock.

Bryan had that stubborn look that scorned surrender. "Then there must be some other way out of the room."

"We made a thorough search of all the rooms on Friday, while looking for the missing guns," Jonas countered. "There are no secret passages, in this room or any other. There is no other way out of this room."

Hatter—who had also searched Jill's room on Friday—confirmed Jonas' assertion with a nod.

"Then you see my problem?" Bryan asked. "Jill did not strangle herself. Yet how could someone enter the room, murder Jill, and leave the room completely sealed—from within? This murder was impossible."

53

"I told you so," Hatter said. "No human could have left the room sealed up like that. But a spirit can pass through walls. It's the only explanation. Even you have to admit that now."

To escape the ghastly scene, the three men had retreated to the drawing room. The dying fire gasped its last light, tinting the room with its eerie amber glow.

Jonas searched Hatter's face for answers but found none. "I don't know how you managed it," he said, "but this spook trick of yours is not going to work."

"Spook trick? Mine? You don't understand. The danger is far from over."

"Don't play games with us, Hatter. When Bryan and I went looking for Bennett, you and Jill were alone with Gideon. One of you killed him. Obviously, it wasn't Jill."

"I was almost one of the victims, myself—remember?" Hatter cried. "Someone tried to poison *me* last night. And nearly succeeded."

"Or that's what we're supposed to think. Isn't it interesting that the killer poisoned you and Carter at the same time, yet only Carter died? Unless, of course, you were intentionally given a nonlethal dose."

"You think *I* did it? Why would I do that? Why poison myself, risk my own life?"

"To divert suspicion from yourself. You would appear to be one of the intended victims and would therefore be ruled out as the murderer. So you could go around murdering everyone else without coming under suspicion—or scrutiny."

"And you weren't really risking your life," Bryan added, "since you were controlling the dose."

"But my motive," Hatter protested. "What motive do I have to kill all of you?"

"That," Jonas said, "is what I believe Bennett uncovered last night. I overheard him talking to you in the parlor room. He was struck by the similarity of the crimes in your books to real-life crimes. It's not hard to figure out what he was implying. He believed that you had committed those real-life crimes to procure details for the crimes in your books."

"That's preposterous! But even if it were true—"

"What does it have to do with us? You've already admitted that you're working on a new novel. Perhaps this game of 'Nine Man's Murder' is your idea of research for that book. You murder us, then use the details of those murders to fuel the plot."

Hatter, reading his defeat in his captors' eyes, made a futile run for the door. His foes, anticipating the maneuver, intercepted the retreat by cutting off the escape route. The captive struggled savagely against his captors.

"So what do we do with him?" Jonas asked.

"I say we tie him up and watch him all night."

Jonas' drooping head struggled against exhaustion. "We've been through the entire inn, garage, and work shed. Did you see anything we can use to tie him up with? I didn't."

"So what do we do? Just sit here with him, trying to stay awake? Or lock him up somewhere?"

"Please, no," Hatter cried. "I won't be safe. You saw what happened to Jill. Locked doors can't stop this … thing. I promise I won't try anything."

"Well, as reassuring as the promise of a man who's murdered seven people is, think about it: a man crafty enough to kill several people in locked rooms guarded by two men who haven't slept in forty-eight hours? I don't think so, Hatter."

Jonas turned to Bryan. "We tried locking him out. What if we tried locking him *in*?"

"No!" Hatter screamed. "You can't do that. You'll be signing my death warrant. You can keep me in, but you can't keep It out."

"There's no sense arguing with him, Jonas. Let's just lock him up."

The question was, where? All of the rooms had doorknobs allowing their doors to be locked—and unlocked—from the inside. All except the library, the only room that could be locked and unlocked solely from the outside. Hatter resisted futilely their efforts to drag him toward the carpeted prison. When they released him in the library, he fell to the floor like a crumpled piece of paper.

All of the library windows were picture windows that could not be opened. The only exit was the door—there were no secret passageways. The men knew, from their search the day before, that beyond the door opposite the north windows lay a storage closet that led nowhere.

"You're going to spend the night here in the library," Jonas told Hatter. "The only way out is to break a window, but the entire inn—every door and window—will be locked up. You can get outside, but there will be no way to get back into any other part of Moon's End. The garage and work shed are not attached to the inn, so you can't get to us through either of them. Therefore I suggest you simply make yourself at home."

Jonas fetched an armload of blankets, tossing them onto the carpet at Hatter's feet.

"Looks like you'll be sleeping on the floor tonight." Jonas glanced at the wall heater, then up at a heating vent near the ceiling, too small to accommodate even a small child. "But the room is well-heated, so you'll be warm, if not comfortable. And, more important, *we'll* be safe."

Hatter looked up with a hollow, ghostly laugh. "You fools," he snapped. "That's the one thing you *won't* be. Don't you see? Locked doors can't keep this killer out."

"We're hoping they will keep him *in*," Jonas said dryly.

54

"What now?" Jonas asked. "Do we stay here and guard the door, in case Hatter gets out?"

Bryan shook his head. "Not sure that's a good idea. If he does get out, he may come out armed—we don't know where he hid those guns. And if he's armed, what then?"

But there was a second argument to which neither man was willing to give voice. Even with their main suspect locked up, the thought of falling asleep within easy access of the only other suspect was unlikely to appeal to someone who hadn't slept in two days.

"You're right," Jonas agreed. "We're probably safer locked in our rooms."

"Besides," Bryan added, "we still have to make it through one more day, pitted against someone it would be fatal to underestimate. We really should rest."

Jonas held out the library key. "What about this? What do we do with it?"

Although Hatter was now locked away, each man was reluctant to entrust the key to his companion, yet careful not to volunteer to hold it himself. Nor would it do to leave the key in a place easily accessible to either. A knotty dilemma, which neither offered to untie.

Something other than hunger sent Bryan to the kitchen. There he began packing pots and pans into a large cardboard box from the service porch, while Jonas, intrigued, lent a hand. Together they wrestled the box upstairs.

Bryan found a suitable bedroom. Hatter and Reeve had had rooms connected by a common bathroom with doors locked from the inside by pushing a button. Bryan opened a drawer of Reeve's night table and asked Jonas for the library key. Satisfied that it *was* the library key, identifiable by its distinctive shape, Bryan placed it in the drawer as Jonas watched vigilantly.

Bryan locked, from within, the door between Reeve's room and the hallway, leaned a chair against the doorknob inside the room, and began piling the upside-down cardboard box, pots, and pans in a wobbly tower of kitchenware propped precariously between the chair and door.

"Now, even if either of us were to get past the lock," Bryan explained, "this door could not be opened without toppling over the pots and pans and making a racket that would wake the soundest sleeper."

They placed the key to Reeve's room (which they had tested in Reeve's lock) in a second drawer of the night table, latched the bedroom window, then stepped into the connecting bathroom and made sure that window was locked, as well. Locking the door to Hatter's bedroom from the bathroom side, they entered Hatter's room and shut the door. The entrance to the bathroom was now sealed and could be unlocked only from within, there being no keyhole on Hatter's side of the door.

"I think the key to the library is safe for the night," Bryan said, satisfied that access to Reeve's room, and the library key locked inside it, had been rendered impossible.

Jonas agreed. "And with Hatter now safe and secure, so are we."

IT HAD BEEN the perfect murder. The door had been locked from within, for the key had been found in the room, with no other way into or out of Jill's room. No way to get out of the room and leave it sealed up like that. It could not have happened, and yet it had.

Of course, the same was true of Amanda's murder. How could any of them have gotten to Amanda's room without being observed by at least one of the others? And Hatter, being in the library, had had the greatest challenge: to get past Jonas in the parlor room and Bryan in the billiard room.

Of course, Bryan knew, for every mystery there is a solution.

Every mystery but one—Amanda's behavior earlier that day. Clearly she had worked something out; but what had triggered her suspicions? If Bryan remembered correctly, her odd manner had begun in response to some remark of Jill's. What was it Jill had said? Aside from browbeating Bryan, all Jill had really talked about this weekend had been their graduation assignment. *Nine Man Morris.*

It always seemed to come back to that.

Had some memory about that assignment tipped Amanda off? Amanda had played a relatively small role in it. The day before Julian Hayward fell to his death, Amanda had inspected the scaffolding with Jonas. The next morning she had been in the director's office with William Hayward. Nothing there.

It was something Jill had said.

Bryan tried to shake the fog from his mind as he returned to his room. What specifically had Jill talked about? William Hayward's skill with makeup, his impersonation of the actors. Jill had been questioning William in the makeup department when Adam Burke twisted his ankle and Julian Hayward—substituting for Burke—fell to his death. Earlier that morning she had been on the lot, watching the three-man construction crew finish work on the scaffolding. The scaffolding that had been sabotaged, despite the fact that they had proven it could *not* have been sabotaged.

Wait.

Was it possible? It was incredible … yet it would explain so much.

Thoughts blurred past as Bryan's sluggish mind began to accelerate. If that was indeed what had happened, could the same thing be happening now? After all, the bridge … Two impossible murders. Even the cigarette lighter. Things were beginning to fall into place.

There was really only one way to be sure.

Bryan made a quick detour to Amanda's room. He opened the door and approached the window. Outside the black night pressed its face against the glass pane, eclipsing all but a few pale streaks of moonlight. Bryan extended his hand, as if to caress the cheek of darkness.

Well, what do you know?

He returned to his room and snapped on the light. He saw it at once, lying on the dresser top.

Closing the door behind him, he approached the silver object.

A handgun.

He studied it with interest, turning it thoughtfully in his hand. A Remington Derringer .38 Special. Loaded. The same type of gun as his own. But it was not his own.

It belonged to Jonas.

✗✗✗ 55

THE NEXT MORNING Jonas was surprised to find Bryan in the dining room, indulging a hearty appetite at breakfast.

"You're up early," Jonas observed. "Did you sleep at all?"

"Not really. How about you?"

Jonas shook his head. "Well, I see this crisis hasn't dulled your appetite."

"Today's the day they come for us: Bill and Max. Looks like we made it. We survived."

"I suppose we should let Hatter out."

"Do we have to?"

They carried the ax upstairs to Reeve's room. Bryan turned the doorknob. The door was still locked. With the ax, Jonas chopped a hole in one panel. He reached in and unlocked the door, easing it open to a protest of crashing metal.

They retrieved the library key from the night table drawer. Entering the connecting bathroom, they found the door to Hatter's room still locked. The windows of Reeve's room and the bathroom had remained latched. The key to Reeve's room was still in its drawer.

Downstairs, the library door had remained locked. With the key Bryan unlocked it, cautiously pushing it open. Jonas entered first.

"Wake up, Hatter," he called. "And don't try anything."

No reply. Was Hatter crouched in silence, preparing to spring a deadly ambush?

They found him lying face down on the floor, his head toward the north windows. They knelt beside him warily, at once noting the two red splotches encircling a pair of holes in Hatter's shirt. In disbelief both men confirmed his death.

The library windows were intact and undamaged.

"Shot twice in the back," Jonas observed. "With a silencer, obviously, or we would have heard the shots."

"Body is cold. Clearly shot last night."

"Then Hatter was framed," Jonas concluded. "Jill's murder must have been made to look 'impossible' intentionally, to throw suspicion on Hatter. We were *supposed* to think that Hatter had murdered Jill and tried to make it look like she was killed by a 'ghost.'"

"And when Hatter and Carter were poisoned Friday night, Hatter *was* intentionally given a small dose, but not for the reasons we had thought. It was to make it *look* like Hatter had poisoned himself to ward off suspicion."

"But, Bryan. There are no bullet holes in the library door or windows, so Hatter was not shot from outside. Which means that he was shot from inside the library."

"But we checked the windows. They're not the kind that can be opened. And none of the panes can be removed."

"And the door key could not have been recovered from Reeve's room."

Could the library key have been replaced with a substitute *before* being locked in Reeve's room, so that it never *was* locked in the room? No. Both men had seen it placed in the drawer, and the key found in Reeve's room this morning *had* indeed opened the library door. It was never out of either's sight, from the moment it was removed from its drawer until the library door was unlocked.

In other words, no one could have switched keys last night and then reswitched them this morning.

"There was no way to unlock the library door," Bryan said, "or relock it after Hatter's murder, without that key. But we know the key could not have been removed from Reeve's room."

Jonas watched Bryan through pinprick pupils. "So how was it done? How did the killer get in—and leave the library sealed up?"

"How indeed?"

Jonas frowned. "So that's where we stand, then? Just another impossible murder?"

"The critical point here is that Hatter is dead now."

Jonas glanced first at Hatter's lifeless body, then at Bryan, before speaking.

"Which leaves the two of us."

56

"JUST THE TWO of us," Bryan echoed. His words seemed to hover in the room. For a moment, neither of the two survivors dared say more, or move. In this game, the first move could be the last.

Breaking the stalemate, Bryan marched down the hallway to his room. Jonas followed, watching from the doorway as Bryan produced a suitcase from the closet, tossed it onto the bed, and calmly began piling clothes into it.

"What are you doing?" Jonas demanded.

"Packing." Bryan did not pause to look up. "They're coming for us today, Bill and Max."

"They may be coming," Jonas said, "*but only one of us will be leaving here alive.*"

"Don't make this more difficult than it has to be," Bryan said.

"What are you going to do? Kill me? And then you'll win the game, is that it? But then, you *always* win, don't you, Bryan? Whatever it takes to eliminate the competition. Is that what you've been doing up here? Eliminating the competition?"

"You're envious," Bryan said, "of my abilities as a detective. You had to show you're as good as me. That's the real reason you broke up the partnership, isn't it?"

"I left the partnership because I could no longer sanction your disregard for conscience and fair play. Stealing clients from the competition—"

"And I suppose it's more ethical to try to steal a woman away from your best friend?"

The question filed the sardonic edge off of Jonas' features.

"Jill knew about my affair with that actress," Bryan continued. "Yesterday she called it a 'birthday present.' How did she know I had betrayed her on her birthday, Jonas? *You* are the only one I told."

"She had a right to know, Bryan. *I* cared about her."

"Only after I started going out with her," Bryan said. "This is what *I* think happened. I think you came up here to prove yourself, by being the only one to solve a series of crimes. Because *you* are the one who committed them."

"You're crazy, Bryan."

That's when Jonas saw it: the handgun on the dresser. How careless of Bryan to leave it lying about. If only Jonas could reach it ... but Bryan was nearer than he. The trick was to approach the weapon without calling Bryan's attention to his movements. Which meant Jonas would have to distract him.

Jonas removed the sheet of paper from his pocket and passed it to Bryan. "I assume you're the one who sent me this."

Bryan studied the sheet. "A copy of a Mexican birth certificate. No, Jonas, I didn't even know it existed."

"Right. Of course." Jonas kept his voice calm. "All right, then, let's talk about the murders. Care to explain how those 'impossible' murders were committed? Like Amanda's, for example."

"I've been giving that matter some thought," Bryan said. "You were in the parlor room. I was in the billiard room. I couldn't have left without being seen by you. Likewise, to get from the parlor room to the staircase, you had to pass by the billiard room—where I was. So, if you had gone up those stairs, I couldn't have missed you." Bryan turned his hands palms up. "Therefore, you didn't."

What was this? A confession?

"No," Bryan continued. "When you left the parlor room, you did not head toward the staircase. You went the *other* way—out the front door. It finally occurred to me. The answer had been in plain view the entire time, if only one knew where to look."

"And where was that?"

"In the work shed. Think back. I'm sure you remember what was in there?"

Jonas thumbed through mental photographs of the work shed. "A work bench. Some tools. A shovel ..."

"And an extension ladder. You went outside, got the ladder from the work shed, propped it against the inn wall, and climbed up to the window of Amanda's room. You opened the window, shot her through it—"

"We found Amanda's window locked. How did I open the window, if it was locked?"

"We found it locked, but that doesn't mean it was locked earlier. Maybe Amanda didn't bother locking it, because she didn't fear entry from a second story window. You shot Amanda, locked the window, and left her room through the door, leaving it unlocked—"

"And how did I get back downstairs, passing you in the billiard room without being seen?"

"You didn't. You left through an empty upstairs bedroom window, shimmying down a drainpipe or trellis. Then you returned the ladder to the work shed and crept back into the parlor room undetected."

Jonas nodded. "I'm impressed. Although I can't help but wonder why I didn't just go back out Amanda's window, instead of locking it and risking my life on the drainpipe."

"To conceal how you got into Amanda's room. And preserve your alibi."

"I suppose. Of course, that scenario can be played both ways. You could have left the billiard room through the kitchen and passed outside through the side door to the work shed to get the ladder. The rest would be as you described."

"Except for one thing. You heard me playing billiards the entire time. Which means I never left the billiard room."

"Does it? What about the tape recorder we found? It was in the billiard room at the time. You simply recorded the sounds of your billiard game, then replayed the tape while you left the room. It would *sound* like you were still playing, while you were really upstairs murdering Amanda."

"Stalemate," Bryan said.

Careful, Jonas thought as he inched toward the gun, *careful. Mustn't make any sudden moves. Keep stalling.*

"And how do you explain Gideon's murder?" Jonas continued. "When he was killed, we were both searching for Bennett, far from the inn."

"Were we? It depends on when you think Gideon was murdered. If, for instance, he was killed before we left ..."

"That's impossible. We were all in the drawing room, from the time Gideon left for his room until we went off in search of Ben—" Suddenly Jonas caught up on the twisted path of Bryan's reasoning. "Oh. So that's what you're getting at. Before we went to look for Bennett, we both retrieved a coat from our rooms. There was just enough time for either of us to have paid a quick visit to Gideon. It would have taken only a few minutes."

"And everyone would assume we had left Gideon alive. Neither of us would be suspected."

Keep talking, Jonas.

Bryan continued. "Those two were easy. Care to tackle something a bit more challenging—like Jill's murder?"

Jonas pondered. "Jill was still in love with you. If you had come to her room last night, she would have let you in."

"She'd have been just as likely to let you in. She trusted you. But that's beside the point. The real question is: If she had let someone in, how did he get *out*, leaving the door locked from within?"

Play along, Jonas told himself. *Play along.*

"He couldn't have, of course. Which opens up an intriguing possibility. We found Jill's door locked—but what if Jill *wasn't dead* when her alarm went off? Hatter and I went to get the ax, leaving you alone in front of Jill's room. Suppose she let you in after we had left. And *that's* when you killed her?"

"Aside from the obvious problem of the purpose of her having set the alarm, your theory still leaves us with the same unanswered question. When you returned with the ax, her door was still locked from the inside. How did I leave her room locked from within? Remember, there are only two ways to lock that door. From the inside, by turning the lock on the doorknob and freezing the knob—*after* the door is closed—or from the outside, with the key."

"And we found the key inside the room."

"Which lets out locking the door from the outside. Leaving only the lock on the knob."

"But Jill was strangled to death, so she didn't get out of bed after the killer left, relock the door, then go back to bed to die. The murderer locked that door. After it was closed."

"From inside the room. Freezing the doorknob and trapping himself in the room. So we're back where we started." Bryan grinned. "With the same question. How did the killer get out of the room with the door locked from within?"

The gun was almost within non-suicidal range. *Steady now …*

"You tell me."

Bryan shrugged. "I'm not the one who knows."

That's when Jonas struck. Bryan had turned aside—only for a moment, but that was all the time Jonas had needed to snatch the gun from the dresser top.

"Very careless, Bryan. Not at all like you, to be caught off guard."

"You're not going to use that, Jonas."

"Don't be too sure. If I kill you, it's all over."

"And you win the game."

"Under the circumstances, I can't very well afford to lose, now can I?"

"No, it wouldn't do to lose at your own game."

"My game, eh?" Jonas removed from his pocket a slip of paper. "You dropped this yesterday. Obviously one of us planned to inform the State Licensing Board about you breaking into that director's office fifteen years ago, to steal his files. You were right. The explanation for these murders lies in our graduation assignment on the set of *Nine Man Morris*.

"If the State Board ever found out how you had tried to steal the files the director had refused to give you, they'd take away your license. The only people who knew about that episode were the director, Damien, and his students. If they were silenced, your secret would be safe forever.

"The director may be dead already, for all I know. But you couldn't kill the rest of us, one by one, in a crowded city. The chance of witnesses, or clues left behind, was too great. Besides, a connection between us would soon be drawn, leading straight to you.

"So you lured us up here. No witnesses. No clues. And it looks like we're all victims of a madman, whom you can say you pushed off a cliff before he made you the final victim."

Bryan applauded. "So I killed you all to protect my career—a career vital to my revenge against Paul Templar."

"You had lost Jill. Revenge was all that was left."

"So tell me. Why did I wait fifteen years?"

"Because it never occurred to you that one of us might turn you in. Until you received that note. And then you panicked."

Bryan contracted his brow. "It does make you wonder, doesn't it, who *sent* me the note? Could it, for example, have been you? To provide me with a motive?"

"What—"

"I think you got the idea from the birth certificate—which is *your* motive. One of us had threatened to expose you as an illegal immigrant and get you deported. Only you didn't know which one."

"So I killed everyone? Seems a bit extreme, don't you think?"

"Leaving the country was not part of your game plan. And isn't that what this has been all along—a game? A game that you intend to win, by framing me for the murders and then killing me in 'self-defense.' It's over, Jonas. Give me the gun."

"Stay where you are!" The abrasive sand of every moment spent in the surreal hourglass of this weekend had frayed Jonas' vocal cords, as well as his nerves.

But Bryan pressed on. "You won't shoot me, Jonas."

Jonas disputed the point with a thrust of the gun.

"You don't have the nerve," Bryan taunted.

"What choice do I have?"

"You're bluffing," Bryan said.

Jonas did not understand. Was Bryan purposely antagonizing him, goading him to shoot?

"That's close enough," Jonas warned. "You slipped up, Bryan, and I have no intention of giving you a second chance."

"Then you're going to have to kill me."

Like a panther Bryan leaped for the gun. Jonas pulled the trigger.

57

Jonas stared down at the motionless body, asking himself what he had to do to wake up. He had killed his partner, his friend.

With the gun still dangling from his hand, Jonas staggered into the parlor room. He would have liked to have heard Bryan's explanation for Jill's murder, as well as Hatter's death. Two seemingly impossible murders: in each, a dead body found in a room with the door locked from within and no window that could be opened. No way in, and certainly no way to have left the rooms sealed up so tight.

Jonas placed the gun on an end table near the entrance to the library corridor. Nothing seemed real; the inn seemed suffused with an eldritch light, as if the last three days had dawned and dimmed inside the head of some cosmic lunatic. But now it was finished. The game was over, and he had won.

"Thank God," he muttered aloud, drifting from the end table. "It's over."

He had heard no footsteps. But suddenly, from the corridor entrance behind him, echoed the sound of unearthly laughter.

"Is it?" a voice asked.

58

It was impossible. Should he have checked to make sure Bryan—?

No. The laugh, the voice was not Bryan's.

This couldn't be. Jonas was the only one left. Yet there on the threshold between the parlor room and corridor that led to the downstairs bedrooms and library Jonas caught, out of the corner of his eye, the silhouette of a man brandishing a gun and laughing eerily. It was the deranged laugh of a demon god looking gleefully on the end of the world. Torn between an urge and a fear to see the intruder's face, Jonas slowly turned.

It wasn't possible. He couldn't be seeing what he was seeing.

It was Bennett.

"You're dead," Jonas gasped. "I examined your body myself."

"No," said the man, with a bodiless laugh suggesting that Hatter had been right all along. "It was Bennett whose body you examined." His hand seemed to float toward his face. "Not mine."

Bennett's fingers seized his nose and, as if in a madman's nightmare, ripped it from his face. No blood. Wait … Another, smaller nose lay beneath the first. From his eyes Bennett removed a pair of colored contacts, then he stripped the bushy eyebrows from his forehead. The sideburns followed, then the moustache and beard. From his overalls he removed a handkerchief, with which he began to wipe away the covering makeup.

This face was one Jonas had seen before, not long ago, at Owen's Reef. Beneath the wig that he yanked from his skull sat a head of short black hair belonging to a man to whom Jonas had paid little heed at the time.

"Bill?" Jonas asked, already knowing the answer.

Bill—the driver of the van who had met them at the train station. The man who, with Max, had delivered them to Moon's End. Bill …

"William," the man corrected.

The taunting notes. The wording of the invitation. The reference to the movie, *Nine Man Morris* …

"William Hayward," Jonas concluded. "You don't look anything like you did fifteen years ago."

"Time—particularly the time I spent starving myself in the asylum—has changed me. Along with some cosmetic help." The impostor continued to wipe the makeup from his face.

"Then *you* were behind the whole thing. But why?"

"Why? Isn't it obvious? You 'great detectives' killed my brother."

"Then it wasn't Bryan …"

"*He* thought it was *you*. That was the beauty of my plan."

"So you planted the gun in his room …"

"It was no matter to me who shot whom. Although, frankly, I had figured on him killing you."

The gun. He had forgotten all about it. But now Jonas realized, to his horror, that he had left the weapon lying on the end table beside which Hayward at this very moment stood; while he himself was barely within wishing range. He had to reach that gun without telegraphing his intent to Hayward.

A show of bewilderment would play to Hayward's ego. "Once the bridge blew up, there was no way for you to have crossed the ravine. So you had to have crossed before then. Yet after the explosion, we searched the entire mountaintop—and there were only nine of us. You couldn't have remained hidden from us, yet that's exactly what you appear to have done. How?"

"Yes, you would have to ask. My first step was to determine which of you was closest to me in height and weight. That turned out to be Bennett. The perfect choice, really, because he hated all of you, and I knew I could persuade him to cooperate. In addition, he had changed so much in fifteen years, I knew none of you would recognize him. Which was essential to my plan.

"I paid a visit to Bennett Nash, in the guise of 'Bill,' of course. I planted the idea that each of his former classmates was in a position to learn about his theft of Capaldi's ledger and expose it to the police. I led him to the idea of coming up here to discover what each of you knew. I made him think it was his own idea.

"The 'reunion' had the added advantage of providing a place for Bennett to hide. And, as a final enticement, I proposed the masquerade as Aaron the caretaker. Bennett was hesitant at first, but I sold the plan as the perfect opportunity to pay you all back for the way you had treated him fifteen years ago: I used to watch you all mock him. Bennett was understandably dubious about playing a mute, but I told him it was to ensure that no one would recognize his voice. Of course, that was not the real reason."

"No, of course not. If Bennett had spoken, then after you took his place, we would have been able to tell the difference between your voice and his. It would have given you away."

"I can imitate faces," Hayward said, "but I can't do voices."

"Jill had mentioned that."

Hayward glossed over his limitations. "I provided Bennett with the outfit to wear to the reunion, so I was able to exactly duplicate his attire when I replaced him later. As I spoke to Bennett, I studied his features. When I got home, I was able to draw sketches from memory and make an exact replica of his face, using prosthetics, makeup, and hair."

"But two weeks ago," Jonas protested, "Gideon helped Bennett—the real Bennett—steal Capaldi's ledger from the police. He heard Bennett's voice—and you can't imitate voices. So Gideon must have known that the 'Bennett' at the reunion was an impostor."

Hayward laughed. "I had been following Bennett for weeks, so I knew about the botched theft. After meeting with Bennett, I disguised myself as him and bailed Gideon out of jail. As 'Bennett,' I visited Gideon and told him I had bailed him out. I said that I had reason to believe one of you was responsible for his accident. I offered to join him up here to help him discover the culprit's identity, in exchange for not betraying 'me' to the police. Obviously, I couldn't have him taking Bennett out of the picture, when Bennett was so vital to my plan."

"But Gideon must have known you weren't really Bennett, from your voice."

"He did ask me why I was talking differently. I told him my plan was to pretend to be Aaron the mute caretaker. I laid out the same plan I had laid out for Bennett—with the addition of Aaron later talking—convincing Gideon that we could use the plan to flush out the one responsible for sabotaging that trap door. He wanted so badly to believe it would work, he was willing to try anything.

"But it was essential, I told him, that no one identify me as Bennett, so I needed to disguise my voice. To ensure I didn't accidently slip into my 'real' voice, I had to get into the habit of talking the new way. Gideon was puzzled, but his mind was overwhelmed by the shower of misfortunes that had recently rained upon him."

"But once everyone up here knew you were 'Bennett'—"

"I would no longer need to 'disguise' my voice? By then the murders had begun, and Gideon had already gotten used to me talking this way. Fear and confusion distracted his mind from considering the matter further. It occurred to him once on Friday night, and he started to ask about it when you came along and interrupted.

"Anyway, that was phase one of my plan," Hayward continued. "I had learned all about Damien's trips to Moon's End each winter. Before he came up here, I drove up and cut the phone lines. When

I had contacted Anderson's about getting in touch with Damien at Moon's End, they told me he communicates with no one while up here. So I knew he would never notice the phone line had been cut. After Damien left for the inn, I sent out invitations to the reunion, knowing that Damien could not be reached to deny having sent them.

"Early Friday morning, I came up here, killed Damien, and pushed his car over the cliff, so that you would have no transportation out, should any of you decide to leave before the bridge blew up. I also found and destroyed the short-wave radio. I knew your cell phones would do you no good up here. I met you all later that day at Owen's Reef, as Bill, the truck driver."

"And what about Max?"

"You're getting ahead," Hayward snapped. "As Bill, I pretended to have a cold, talking in a hoarse voice—"

"So we wouldn't recognize it later, when 'Bennett' started talking."

"Not bad, for a detective." Hayward was so self-absorbed, he failed to notice the shrinking distance between himself and Jonas. "Everything went exactly as planned. Bennett showed up dressed in the clothes I had provided. I brought everyone here and left with Max. Once the truck was out of sight, I stopped and got out. I changed into the same clothes Bennett was wearing and made myself up to look like him. Max took off, with instructions to return in three days."

"So that was why it took two people to drive us up here," Jonas muttered. "Someone had to return with the truck later, and it couldn't be you—since you were to be stranded up here with us." *Don't break eye contact*, Jonas reminded himself. *Anchoring Hayward's eyes will keep them from floating toward the gun.*

"I crossed back over the bridge and set the explosive. Then I went to a place where I had arranged to meet with Bennett, to 'give him his next instruction.'"

"I saw him check his watch and leave the inn."

"He was right on schedule. The unsuspecting fool was taken completely by surprise. I killed him before he even knew what was happening."

"We wondered how Bennett could have been caught so completely off guard by the killer, despite the other murders. But when Bennett was killed, there had been no other murders."

Hayward nodded. "I buried him twenty paces east of a tree I had marked, right there in the snow—"

"Making it impossible to determine how long he had been dead. We thought Bennett had been killed on Saturday morning, when 'he' had disappeared. But he had actually been dead since *the day before*. Without the snow preserving him, we'd have known that Bennett had been dead since Friday afternoon, and would have realized that the Bennett who had been alive on Friday night and Saturday was an impostor. And still at large."

"You had to believe he'd been dead for only six or seven hours, when in fact he'd been dead for over twenty-four." Hayward indulged in a triumphant pause. "After killing Bennett, I went to the inn, dressed as Bennett had been dressed, and took his place. That was why—though there were *ten* of us on the mountaintop—you never found a tenth person. I took the place of the *ninth* person. The real ninth person was buried in the snow. The perfect hiding place.

"As a mute, Bennett had not spoken up to that point. So, when 'he' later began talking, I did not have to worry about imitating his voice. All I had to do was make sure I never got too close to any of you, so that no one would notice any wig lines, seams, or other evidence of makeup."

"That's why you kept your distance from everyone. But why actually go ahead with the theft of the guns? I thought that had simply been a pretext for Bennett's benefit, to lure him to the reunion. Why actually go through with it, once he was dead?"

"I knew I might not be able to keep up the charade of being mute. In fact, I *wanted* to talk, to control everything that went on, if necessary. So I needed an explanation for why Bennett had been pretending to be mute."

"And that explanation was to create a mystery none of us could solve: a scream no one could have made and guns that had disappeared equally impossibly."

"With the added benefit of rendering you all defenseless."

That was when Hayward noticed the gun.

Jonas' wildcat leap was no match for Hayward's tactical advantage. Left hand clutching the gun like a cattle prod, Hayward forced his victim deeper into the parlor room, as he tucked his own weapon into his waistband, undoubtedly amused with the irony of shooting Jonas with his own gun.

"That was a mistake," Hayward said.

Jonas tried to forestall the inevitable with a raised palm. "Wait. Surely you're not going to kill me without telling me how you pulled off the murders?"

As Jonas had hoped, Hayward succumbed to vanity. "Why not? I poisoned Carter's dinner Friday night and gave Hatter a nonlethal dose. I knew that would cause you to suspect Hatter eventually.

"That afternoon I had climbed up the trellis to Amanda's window. While she was showering I stole her room key. Unfortunately, on the way down I broke a couple of wooden slats—"

"Jill and I noticed them."

"So I knew the trellis was no longer safe. From then on I used the ladder from the shed. That night I planted the gun in Amanda's room and her room key in Reeve's room, along with the fire poker and note that would bring Reeve to Amanda's room—and to his death. Later that night I attacked Amanda on the staircase, to set up Reeve's murder.

"On Saturday morning it was time for Bennett to disappear. I left the inn, still dressed precisely as Bennett had been dressed when I had killed him the day before. When you found the real Bennett's body, he would be attired exactly as he had been when 'he' left the inn Saturday morning. I made certain I was observed leaving, to ensure that Bennett's body would eventually be sought and found. I didn't want you looking for him later, and finding me."

"That's why you marked the grave. To make sure we'd find the body."

"Obviously. Later, it was time to kill Amanda. She had locked her door and window—"

"Then how did you get into her room?"

Hayward chuckled. "The same way I broke into Reeve's room. After I killed Damien on Friday morning, I made a slight modification to Amanda's window latch. I removed the inner spring and pin. Even with the latch pushed all the way into the locked position, the window is not locked. There's no pin to hold it in place. A simple push will open the window, even in the locked position. Amanda only *thought* she had locked the window."

Why didn't I think of that? Jonas asked himself.

"I used the ladder from the work shed to climb up to Amanda's window. I pushed opened the 'locked' window and shot her. I unlocked her door and left through the window, leaving it 'locked.' But before I killed her, I used the shovel to mark the spot where I had buried Bennett."

"But why masquerade as Bennett, only to end the charade later?"

"Don't you see? Only as one of you could I control everything. Besides, there was no place on the mountaintop to hide. Eventually you would search the area, and I would be found. The only safe hiding place was as one of you.

"But as the list of suspects dwindled, it would be more difficult to get away with murder. With fewer people to keep an eye on, I would be too closely watched. But if I—as Bennett—were to die, you would all be focusing on one another—an outsider having already been ruled out—leaving me free to go about my plan unseen, my presence unsuspected.

"Amanda's window was not the only one I had tampered with. There were others: Reeve's, Bryan's, Gideon's, Carter's, and yours. After killing Amanda, I hid in Carter's room until you and Bryan went off in search of Bennett. While you two were out finding his body, I went back outside through Carter's window and climbed through Gideon's."

"And you managed to enter Gideon's room without leaving him time to get out a cry for help—"

"Because I had broken into the room earlier, while he was out with the rest of you, and drugged his juice. When I later climbed through his window, he was fast asleep. I killed him easily and unlocked the door—since you were to suspect Hatter or Jill—and hid in the library. Then, when Jill raced out of her room in response to your discovery of Gideon's body—leaving her door unlocked—I slipped into her room and hid in her closet—"

"So that's how you murdered Jill in a sealed room. You were already *in* the room when the door was locked, and you managed to leave the room sealed up … because you never left."

"I had substituted Jill's medication with sleeping pills before hiding in the closet. Once she was asleep, I crept out and strangled her. I then set her alarm to rouse you all—the next murder had to take place at night, when you would not all be together, so I had to get you out of your locked rooms—and returned to the closet. There were only three of you left—Hatter, Bryan, and yourself—and you had all gathered in Jill's room. The notion of an outsider had already been dismissed, so I knew you wouldn't search for anyone else. I waited safely in the closet until the three of you left the room. While you were in the drawing room, I planted your gun in Bryan's room. When he had rushed out of his room in response to Jill's alarm, he did not have the presence of mind to lock his door."

"And then?"

"I figured you would suspect Hatter and lock him in the only room that could not be unlocked from the inside: the library. Which is exactly what you did. I was already waiting in the library storage closet. I shot Hatter a short time later, while his back was turned."

"That explains the position in which we found Hatter's body. Face down, his head toward the north windows—which are across the room from the storage closet. His *back* had thus been to the storage room—and he had been shot in the back. That should have told us he had been shot from the storage closet."

"The rest *you* helped me with," Hayward continued. "By planting your gun in Bryan's room, I simply allowed you both to fight it out between yourselves. Now all that's left is to kill you …"

"You can't hope to get away with it," Jonas warned desperately.

"I already have. All of the bodies will be buried in the snow. When

Max arrives with help this afternoon, all they'll find is a lone vacationer stranded on a mountaintop."

"But Max knows how many were brought here."

"Of course he does. He's in on it. A fellow inmate from Lakeview. Crazy as a loon. He knows the bridge is blown up. That's why he's bringing help. I will be rescued, and no one will ever know that anyone else had been up here. Even if they eventually find the bodies, there's nothing to tie William Hayward to this gathering. I worked out every detail flawlessly."

"Every detail but one."

The words had not come from Jonas. They had materialized behind William Hayward.

Swiftly the gunman turned to face what should have been an empty corridor behind him. In the entrance to the parlor room Jonas and Hayward could see the shape of a man leaning casually against the door jamb.

"Bryan," Jonas gasped.

59

"But I shot you," Jonas protested. "At close range. I *couldn't* have missed."

"Well, *I* won't miss," William Hayward promised just before pulling the trigger. An explosion knocked every complacent thought in the room off its feet; yet Bryan remained standing. Hayward squeezed the trigger again and again, knowing his aim had not strayed—yet had not reached its target, somehow.

With a wisp of a grin, Bryan reached into his pocket, withdrawing a clenched fist that he held outstretched before him. His fingers unfurled to reveal several shells.

"Blanks," Bryan explained. "I got them from Jonas at the train station." Again he dipped into his pocket. "Now *this*," he added, removing a handgun, "is loaded. I borrowed it from Amanda's room on Friday night."

"So *that's* how it disappeared," Hayward muttered.

"Then that battle between us," Jonas asked Bryan. "You staged the whole thing?"

"It was the only way to flush out the murderer. And of course, if my theory was incorrect—and you *were* the murderer, Jonas—it was to my advantage that you think me dead."

"I don't believe it," Hayward exclaimed. "You *couldn't* have known."

"For a long time," Bryan admitted, "I didn't. You came quite close to getting away with it."

"What gave him away?" Jonas asked.

"It was a number of little things, none of them conclusive in itself. For instance, one of the murderer's notes had mentioned writing a book about us and being sued for 'slander.' Of course, anyone with a legal background knows that you wouldn't be sued for slander, but *libel*. The thing is—and I pointed this out at the time—Damien gave us all a very thorough legal background.

"This was my first indication that the murderer was not really a detective—at least not one trained by Damien. But, as I said, it was not conclusive in itself. However, I did begin to notice that the murderer's notes made liberal use of some technical film terms: 'premiere,' 'spotlight,' 'scenario,' 'fade to black.' That, in conjunction with the reference to the movie *Nine Man Morris*, made me start to suspect that our killer might be someone involved in the film industry—specifically, someone who had worked on *Nine Man Morris*—masquerading as a detective.

"And when Jill reminded us about William Hayward's abilities as a makeup artist, I began to consider the possibility of a deranged William Hayward—who had recently been released from an asylum—having disguised himself as one of us, to avenge his brother's death. In other words, that one of us was an impostor. The question was, which one? And that, Hayward, was where you gave yourself away."

"How?"

"Damien had been stabbed through the aorta, yet the wound had scarcely bled—a fact to which I myself alluded. But a knife wound through a major artery—especially one near the surface of the skin—*should* have bled profusely. To a trained detective this could only have meant one thing: Damien was already dead when he was stabbed. This view was supported by the blow to his head that we found. The killer had knocked Damien out first, and, not realizing that the blow had been fatal, he then stabbed his victim.

"But as Bennett, you made a grave mistake. You expressed the belief that Damien had died of the knife wound, when you pointed out how quickly the victims had died. That suggested to me that Bennett was no detective.

"This conclusion was reinforced by other things. On several occasions you—that is, 'Bennett'—had used terms normally reserved for the film industry. When we were trying to interpret the murderer's second note, you talked about getting it right 'on the first take.' You also spoke of 'standing in' for me with Jill. This suggested a background and training that had more to do with film than private investigation."

"It all sounds pretty flimsy to me, West."

"And so it was. That is, if it hadn't been for a more substantial discrepancy. One that had been bothering me for some time. The detonator."

"What was wrong with it?"

"We had all assumed that the explosive that had blown up the bridge had been set by the murderer on Friday morning, after he had killed Damien. But, if you remember, it had rained heavily before we left the train station Friday afternoon. Later we found the detonator behind a rock—uncovered. It was housed in a balsa wood box.

"Balsa wood absorbs water readily. If the box had been placed there on Friday morning, before the afternoon rain, exposed as we found it, it should have been waterlogged when we discovered it. But it was bone dry—as you noted, Jonas. The entire day had been overcast: There had been no sun to dry it out. Which meant the detonator could not have been placed there before the rain. It was planted *after* the rain—and therefore, after we arrived. Planted by one of us.

"But the only one of us to have left the inn between our arrival and the explosion was Bennett. So there, I reasoned, was proof that Bennett had set the charge—as he was the only one who could have—and was our man."

"But that's not the way it happened," Hayward objected. "When Bennett left the inn, he went straight to meet me—and I had already set the explosive, after Max had driven off and I had recrossed the bridge."

"Yes, I realize that now. But at the time, I didn't question my conclusion—that is, until we found Bennett's body. Which was when it all fell apart—there went my prime suspect. I must hand it to you, Hayward, that threw me completely off course. And it took me a long time to get back on track.

"After a while, however, the logical conclusion began to force itself on me. If the explosive had been set after we arrived, and not by Bennett or the rest of us, then there was only one other possible explanation—a *tenth* person had to have planted it after our arrival at Moon's End. Of course, it took quite a while for me to come to this conclusion—since we had already ruled out a tenth person.

"It wasn't until I confronted something else that had been troubling me that I began to take this theory more seriously. From the beginning, I had felt there was something about the reunion that was not quite right—aside from the fact that the guests were all being murdered. It wasn't until much later that I realized what that was.

"If the reunion had all been a sham—if Damien had never sent those invitations—then what had Bill been doing at Owen's Reef? Who had sent a truck to meet us at the train station, if Damien hadn't? And if 'Aaron' was just a masquerade—if Damien had never really hired a caretaker named Aaron—how could Bill have known about him? Clearly Bill was in on it—the elusive tenth person."

"Unless Bill had been an innocent dupe," Jonas suggested. "That is, what if the murderer had arranged with Bennett to masquerade as Aaron, and then simply hired Bill, telling him about Aaron?"

"Then how did Bill *recognize* Aaron? As the mute Aaron, Bennett never uttered a word—never identified himself as Aaron—yet Bill knew him on sight."

"The murderer described Aaron to Bill."

"And how did the murderer know what Aaron (that is, Bennett) looked like? As Bennett later told us (falsely, it turned out), he had never met the murderer. Bennett had been given his instructions *over the telephone*. If the murderer never met Bennett (that is, Aaron), how could he have described him to Bill?"

"Bill could have been told what Aaron would be wearing," Jonas suggested.

"Bennett wore a gray raincoat and rain hat completely covering his clothes. So did Hatter. Yet Bill picked Bennett out immediately, though Hatter had arrived first. No, Bill was not an innocent dupe hired by the murderer," Bryan continued. "He was part of the plot, the mysterious tenth person. And if so, then perhaps *he* was William Hayward.

"Jill had unknowingly hinted at this when she recognized Bill at Owen's Reef. She had spent time at the Lakeview sanitarium, where William Hayward had been committed." Bryan studied Hayward. "She must have seen you there after your hunger strike had altered your appearance—so she did not recognize you as William Hayward in the asylum. Years later, however, at Owen's Reef, you naturally looked familiar.

"Of course, there was one major objection to the tenth-person theory," Bryan continued. "There were only nine of us on the mountaintop. A search had ruled out a tenth person. It wasn't until I finally put together some clues that had been staring me in the face that I realized the truth.

"Do you remember that while you were disguised as Bennett, Jill spilled wine on your white overalls? That was a critical oversight on your part. Because when we found Bennett's body, he was still wearing those same white overalls—and they were spotless. There *should* have been a wine stain on the pants leg—like the one on yours now." Bryan indicated a red stain on the leg of Hayward's white trousers. "But of course, Bennett was already dead and buried before the wine-spilling incident took place.

"Unfortunately, none of this occurred to me at the time. Once it did, however, the implications were clear. The man we had found buried in the snow was not the same one Jill had spilled wine on. There were two Bennetts.

"The indications had been plain enough, if only I had read the signs. At Owen's Reef you (as Bill) had produced a cigarette and asked for a light. Odd: a man who carries cigarettes but no way to light them. But then, you had dropped your cigarette lighter at Moon's End that morning, when you murdered Damien.

"It was that lighter that we gave Bennett—the real Bennett—when we found it. When, a short time later, he left to meet you and you killed him, you buried him—unknowingly—with the lighter in his pocket. That was why, when we later asked you about the lighter, after you had taken Bennett's place, you had no idea what we were talking about—because it was not *you* to whom the lighter had been given. You hastily improvised a story about having lost it. You can imagine my confusion when the lighter ended up *back* in Bennett's pocket when we found his body. Of course, it had been there all along.

"That was another clue I had overlooked. If you give a right-handed person an object, he'll take it in his right hand and put it in his right pocket. But we found the lighter in the *left* front pocket of Bennett's pants. And he wore his wristwatch on his *right* arm.

"You see, Bennett was *left-handed*—while you, on the contrary, are *right-handed*. I've seen you favor your right hand. Another indication that the left-handed Bennett who had departed the inn Friday afternoon was not the same as the right-handed one who returned.

"This, in turn, explained why Aaron had manifested two distinctly different personalities—one timid and uncertain, the other confident. It was as if there had been two different Aarons, as indeed, there had been two different Bennetts playing him. The real Bennett was the insecure one; you were the confident one. If only I had realized this earlier.

"Eventually, however, I began to fit the pieces together, until I finally formed a picture consistent with the facts. Bill, whom Jill had recognized as William Hayward without having realized it, had killed Bennett shortly after our arrival at Moon's End and had taken his place."

Some lunatic alchemy transmuted Hayward's defeat into a laugh of deranged triumph. "But you figured it out too late—too late to save the others. None of you could stop me from repaying you all for the roles you played in my brother's death: Carter, for having proposed the graduation assignment in the first place; Damien, for having assigned it." He turned savagely upon Bryan. "You, Bryan, for putting everyone back on the case after Reeve had implicated Adam Burke by planting Burke's ring in the sabotaged stunt car. The affair would have ended then and there if it hadn't been for your meddling.

"Then there was Reeve's bungling the attempt to frame Burke. Hatter and Gideon had been assigned to guard the set, yet had failed to keep out the saboteur." Here Hayward turned to Jonas. "You, Jonas, had inspected the scaffolding with Amanda, yet had overlooked the sabotage—"

"How could they have found anything," Bryan asked, "when the set hadn't yet been tampered with? The same goes for Hatter and Gideon. And while we're at it, aren't you leaving out a major contributor to your brother's death—the one who actually sabotaged the set? *You*, William."

Hayward stood speechless.

"It had always struck me as peculiar," Bryan explained, "that the accidents involving your brother had all been relatively harmless. They were never even potentially life-threatening—"

"You're forgetting the one that killed him," Hayward protested.

"But that's precisely the point. It was *Adam Burke* who was supposed to have performed that stunt. It was only an unforeseen turn of events that caused him to be switched at the last moment with your brother. It was almost as if Julian had never been meant to be injured by the accidents. But when Burke was the intended target, the tampering took on a much deadlier nature.

"Adam Burke was going to replace your brother as Hollywood's premier stunt man. You were outraged and set out to prevent it. You could have undermined Burke's stunts to make him look bad, but then your brother might have been suspected, if sabotage was discovered.

"So instead you sabotaged Julian's stunts, hoping that Burke would be accused of trying to eliminate the competition. Of course, you were careful to make sure your brother was never actually in jeopardy.

"You had hoped to have Adam Burke blacklisted as a stuntman; but when that plan failed, you turned to more drastic measures. You tried to get rid of Burke permanently, by sabotaging a dangerous stunt. The scaffolding scene.

"Unfortunately—for you—Burke twisted his ankle when Bennett removed the staircase from his trailer. Julian had to replace Burke at the last minute. Only you didn't find out on time, because Jill had detained you in the makeup department."

"I figured out Bennett's role in Burke's accident," Hayward explained, "as well as Jill's responsibility for what ensued. I took great pleasure in repaying their contributions to my brother's death."

"Now Gideon's accident," Bryan continued. "That was your doing as well, wasn't it?"

"I went to sabotage the set that night. But Gideon was guarding it. I had to get him out of the way. I rigged the trap door and made a noise to draw him in that direction. I had hoped the fall would render him unconscious. I didn't know he would end up paralyzed."

Bryan frowned, more at himself than at Hayward. "I should have realized your role in Julian's death long ago, and I didn't. But someone else did."

"Amanda," Jonas said.

"It was something Jill had mentioned yesterday that tipped Amanda off. Amanda had told us—while Jill was out of the room—that she had been in the director's office on the morning of Julian's fatal fall, when the director received a telephone call. One of the three crew members who were to have completed work on the scaffolding was sick and would not be coming in that day. No replacement had been available.

"Yet later, Jill told us that she had watched *three* members of the construction crew finish the job." Bryan's eyes glowed like those of a cat crouched to pounce. "There *should* have been only two. I think

Amanda put things together and realized that one of those three crew members had been an impostor."

Bryan turned toward Hayward. "You had failed to sabotage the set the night before. It had been guarded regularly before and after Gideon's accident, so you couldn't get near it. But you were in the director's office with Amanda when that call came through the next morning. That's when you saw your opportunity. You disguised yourself as one of the construction crew—it was the only way you could get onto the set. Everyone simply saw three construction workers, as usual. You sabotaged the scaffolding as the work was being completed. It's the only time the set could have been tampered with.

"Amanda deduced that the third crew member had been you. You were the only other person in the director's office that morning, besides the director, and therefore the only one who knew about the sick construction worker. That was probably what she had wanted to talk to Jonas about yesterday. She may have conjectured, as I later did, that if disguise had been involved in Julian's death, it may also have played a part up here.

"But it was already too late. Because after Jill mentioned the three construction workers, Amanda began acting strangely. You noticed that and figured out why. You couldn't take any chances. You had to silence her before she could share her suspicions with anyone else. That's why she was killed ahead of schedule."

"Julian was never going to see me independent: not as long as he lived." William's body seemed to go limp, as if dangling from strings it could not cut. "But all by myself I punished the people responsible for his death."

"*You* were responsible for his murder, William," Bryan said. "*You* sabotaged the set."

"It was an accident," Hayward insisted. "Murder is killing with intent."

"That set was deliberately sabotaged," Bryan said. "*You* killed your brother, not us."

"No." Hayward was strangely calm.

"You murdered him," Jonas insisted.

"No!" Hayward roared. He whipped the handgun from his pocket and aimed it at Jonas. But before Hayward could pull the trigger, Bryan fired his own weapon. Hayward fell at Jonas' feet. Warily, Jonas examined the motionless body. Hayward was dead.

"I owe you one," Jonas said. "But what do we do now?"

"We wait to be rescued."

"That's not what I meant. We have no proof that all those people buried in the snow weren't murdered by us."

"That's why I took some precautions." Bryan reached behind and produced the cassette tape recorder they had found two days earlier. "We've got Hayward's confession on tape."

"I underestimated you," Jonas said. His eyes dropped. "Sorry about killing you."

A dismissive hand sliced through the air like a sharpened sword through twisted rope. "You can't undo things you didn't do to begin with."

"I thought you were trying to—." Jonas shook his head. "We're a lot alike, you know. With a lot in common."

But Bryan said nothing. Instead, he removed the cord from around his neck.

"What are you doing?" Jonas asked.

"A final gift to Jill."

"You're giving up the crusade against her father?"

"Actually, I'm thinking of retiring. Spending more time with Prissy. Maybe she can help me raise a little girl I'm thinking of adopting."

"Sounds very domestic," Jonas said. "But as for retiring, it seems a shame to break up such a good act without giving it just one more chance …"

ACKNOWLEDGMENTS

I wish to acknowledge my debt to Christian Alighieri, the "invisible author." (He's the one who put the period *inside* the quotes of this acknowledgment.)

ABOUT THE AUTHOR

Eric Keith is a former puzzle designer for a company that created logical games and puzzles. His experience with devising devious twists and turns of logic has helped him create intricately plotted murder mysteries. He and his wife Marcia live in San Diego. He can be reached via email at **EricKeith@MysteriesWithTwists.com**, and his co-star in the photo is Pamplemousse.